BROOKS (SPECIAL FORCES: OPERATION ALPHA)

GOLD TEAM - BOOK 1

RILEY EDWARDS

Dear Readers,

Welcome to the Special Forces: Operation Alpha Fan-Fiction world!

If you are new to this amazing world, in a nutshell the author wrote a story using one or more of my characters in it. Sometimes that character has a major role in the story, and other times they are only mentioned briefly. This is perfectly legal and allowable because they are going through Aces Press to publish the story.

This book is entirely the work of the author who wrote it. While I might have assisted with brainstorming and other ideas about which of my characters to use, I didn't have any part in the process or writing or editing the story.

I'm proud and excited that so many authors loved my characters enough that they wanted to write them into their own story. Thank you for supporting them, and me!

READ ON!

Xoxo

Susan Stoker

BEFORE YOU BEGIN

Thank you for purchasing Brooks. I'm beyond thrilled to once again write in Susan Stoker's Special Forces: Operation Alpha universe. I've been a fan of Susan's for many years and have read every book she's published (multiple times.) While I've tried my hardest to stay true to her original characters (because, *hello,* they are already awesome) I am not Susan, I wrote them as I, the reader, experienced them.

I want fans of Susan to feel like they're visiting old friends when they see her beloved characters. I hope I've done them justice. But please remember, I've taken some liberties.

In Brooks, I use Susan's characters from her new Legacy SEAL series: Rocco, Ace, Gumby, Phantom, Bubba, and Rex. I've also borrowed plot elements from *Securing Caite* and bad guys, too. You can certainly read Brooks as a standalone but I recommend reading *Securing Caite* first.

And of course, The King of All Things Cyber, John "Tex" Keegan makes an appearance.

I hope you enjoy the world I've created for you as much as I loved writing it.

Sign up for the **Riley's Rebels** mailing list to receive a **FREE COPY of Unbroken** and stay up to date on releases, sales, and giveaways.
https://www.subscribepage.com/rileyedwardsfreebook

For Susan.

Thank you for giving us, your adoring readers, such wonderful characters.

PROLOGUE

Zane Lewis

The incessant ringing and vibrating of my phone pulled me from a deep, sated sleep. I angrily snatched my phone off the nightstand and without checking the caller ID, I entered in my ten-digit security code and answered.

"Zane," I growled.

It was two in the goddamn morning, someone had better be bleeding or missing body parts.

"We have a problem." John "Tex" Keegan cut right to the chase, one of the many things I liked about the man. That and he had to be hands-down the best computer geek I'd ever met. Though I'd never call the former SEAL a *geek* to his face.

"Of course we do." I glanced over at my beautiful wife as she stirred in her sleep. Ivy sighed and rolled to her side. The sexy sound made my cock jerk. Not even an hour ago, she had made that same sweet sound after I brought her to orgasm with my mouth and fingers. Regretfully, I slid out of bed and grabbed a pair of sweats on my way out of the bedroom and down the stairs. "What kind of problem?"

"Tatiana Jones called me when she found out Gold Team was in Bahrain."

There was so much to process from that one simple statement.

"At two in the fucking morning?"

"It's ten a.m. in Bahrain."

"Tatiana Jones is in Bahrain?"

It was taking longer for my sleep-muddled mind to track than it should have.

"Yep. And she wants reassurances that the team will not be an issue for her."

"What the actual fuck? I thought she retired. Found herself a nice man to drive off into the sunset with. Oh, wait, I forgot she married that asshole Monroe. Bet that ended badly."

Ivy would've given me shit if she'd heard me making smartass comments about the failure of someone's marriage. Or maybe not if she knew what a douche James Monroe was. He was an embarrassment to the Special Operations community and a shit husband from what I'd heard.

"After she finally got shot of Monroe, she went back to work," Tex informed me.

"A new company, or did she go back to her previous employer?"

"New. She's running solo now."

Well, fuck me running. There was nothing I could do but agree to the meet.

"Would you mind putting together any intel you can dig up on her and pass it to Declan?"

"That's a joke, right? There's nothing out there I can put in a workup for the team. And even if I could dig something up, I wouldn't ever divulge it in a report."

"Would you take a meet with an unknown?" I asked.

"Hell, no."

"Right. Dec's gonna want a dossier. I don't care how barebones it is. We have to give him something. And it should be a quick meet and greet. Gold Team will only be in Bahrain a few more days, tops. In and out." Tex's deep rumbling chuckle gave me pause. I'd only ever heard the man laugh a few times.

"What's funny?"

"You've seen her, yeah?"

"Shit."

Tex's chuckle turned into a deep belly laugh. "Good luck."

"Ass," I mumbled. "Thanks for the heads-up."

"Anytime. I'll have something for you by morning."

"Night."

I disconnected and continued to stare out the floor-to-ceiling windows, overlooking the marina down below. My gut told me this wasn't going to end well.

I actually felt sorry for Declan Crenshaw. It wasn't too long ago I'd given him the Gold Team. He'd been restless since he'd quit the CIA and came to work for me. I thought giving him his own team to lead would help him work out some of his issues before he burrowed in any deeper. Years of deep undercover work could fuck with a man. He hadn't shared what he'd seen or done, and I didn't push.

Tatiana wouldn't be an issue for Declan. He'd made it clear he didn't want to settle down and find a woman. Though, neither did I, until Ivy. One look at her and all bets were off. No, Declan wouldn't have any interest in the woman. Dec had also revealed when he was ready to find a woman, he wanted a delicate wallflower. There was nothing delicate about Tatiana.

"Whatcha doing?" Ivy asked.

I heard her the minute her feet hit the top of the stairs. Even if I hadn't been trained to detect the quietest of sounds, I would've known she was in the room. Every part of me was aware of my wife.

"Thinking," I told her when her arms wrapped around me from behind.

"About?"

"How good it's going to feel when I press you against this window and slide inside of you."

"Really? That's what had you so deep in thought?"

"Yep."

I had Ivy in my arms, legs around my waist, and her body balanced against the window before she could ask anymore questions.

"I love you, Zane."

"I love you, Ivy."

With my wife's heat surrounding me, all thoughts of the Gold Team and Tatiana Jones flew out the window.

They'd figure it out. Surely, the group of five former special operations soldiers could handle one tiny woman. Even if that woman had the reputation of being one of the best spies the CIA had ever trained before she went rogue.

CHAPTER 1

I knew three things as absolute fact: the woman sitting across the table from me was a liar, her need for a bullshit cover story was not my business, and she had the best pair of legs I'd ever seen. The shiny black fuck-me-heels drew attention from her calves all the way up to her toned thighs. *Hot damn.* Yep, I had no business checking the woman out, yet there I was analyzing her, and completely distracted by a great set of calves and sexy heels.

The dossier my boss, Zane Lewis, had sent to the team said her name was Tatiana Jones. Declan, Max, Thad, Kyle, and myself had combed through the sparse documents. Supposedly she worked for the UN as a Political Affairs Officer. The job title fell under the office of counter-terrorism. The department was legit, she may have even been on their payroll, but her body language and knowing gaze screamed 'operative.'

We'd barely entered her office when she'd made it clear she wasn't pleased we were in the Kingdom of

Bahrain. She knew why we were in the country. We had a singular objective, follow the money trail and click another piece of the puzzle together. A simple recon expedition that should've in no way hindered the UN task force's counterterrorism strategy. Unless she was bullshitting. Which she was.

"I've been in contact with Mr. Lewis. He briefed me on the Militrix transoceanic cabling contract in the Gulf of Bahrain. My divers inspected the area around the King Fahd Causeway. There's no cabling." It sounded as if she'd practiced her speech, wanting us out of her office as quickly as possible.

"Your divers?" I interrupted.

Why would a Political Affairs Officer have divers on hand and at her disposal? *She wouldn't.*

"Yes. Mine. The area is clear."

Interesting. In her desperation to keep us away from what she was working on, she'd slipped up. Rookie mistake. Maybe she wasn't as well-trained as I'd originally thought. Maybe she was a junior agent.

"If you don't mind, I'd like to take a look myself," I pushed.

I didn't need her permission, nor did I really care to get it. I simply wanted to keep her talking. Tatiana Jones and whatever she was doing in the region had zero impact on my mission, yet I wanted to know. Actually, I wanted to know more about her in general, which was crazy.

"There's no need. I have the utmost trust in—"

"Right. You may, but I don't. And all due respect, I trust but verify."

Tatiana leaned back and eyed me with a critical stare. Yep. I'd been correct and she was getting ready to show her hand. I doubted many people cut her off mid-sentence. I'd also bet she gave the orders, and wasn't pleased when she had to follow them herself. There was a glint in her dark eyes that was sexy as hell. A flash of fire and icy annoyance. *Yeah, she could order me around anytime.* The look made me want to piss her off some more just so I could see it again.

"I know all about your verification process, Mr. Miller. I'm also well-acquainted with men like you."

Here we go. I'd hit a hot button topic for her. Overbearing daddy or husband maybe.

Men like you… I wanted to tell her she'd never met a man like me and that was a goddamn guarantee.

"Oh, yeah? And what kind of man am I, Doll?"

"An overachiever. Demolitions expert. Divemaster. Low and high-altitude jumpmaster. Rappel Master. Fast Rope Master."

She was missing a few of my quals, and I had to fight the urge to school her on all things Brooks Miller. Like how good I was with my hands, I was top of my class in close quarter combat. My hand techniques were the best around.

And it was more than me knowing hundreds of ways to kill a man without breaking a sweat.

"Glad to see you've done your homework. Unfortunately the work-up we received on you was only a paragraph. There was nothing listing *your* accomplishments."

"My accomplishments aren't important. The only thing that's imperative is you don't fuck up my op."

Interesting. She'd laid her cards on the table. The question remained, was it intentional, or had she fucked up?

"Well, Miss Jones. It is *Miss*, correct? We wouldn't want to get in your way. I'll take a quick look around this afternoon and hopefully in a few days we'll be on our way."

"It's actually *none-of-your-business*," Tatiana sparred. "I'll take you out there myself. Tomorrow, oh-five-hundred."

"You'll take me out?"

"Good to know all your combat tours haven't diminished your hearing."

"What do you know about diving?"

"You're not the only one with special quals, friend. If we're done, I have shit to do. I was promised you guys wouldn't be an issue."

I wanted to keep pushing the spunky woman, but Declan looked like he was ready to stroke out. We'd been warned not to piss Tatiana off. While the details about her were sketchy at best, the report was clear she knew and had worked with some very important people.

"There will be no issues from us," Declan confirmed. "Recon and out."

"Good. I have something scheduled in less than a week. I'd prefer you were gone by then."

"Ah. You're kicking us out of your country?" Unable to stop myself I dramatically covered my chest.

Tatiana shook her head, not the least bit amused by my behavior. "With big egos, comes bigger mouths," she mumbled. "Have a nice afternoon, gentlemen. Mr. Miller, I'll see you at the docks off fifty-ninth, slip fifteen."

All I needed was a few hours and I'd wipe the disdain off her pretty face. It wouldn't take long to show her that my big ego was hard-earned confidence and not bullshit talk.

Tatiana didn't wait for us to stand before she took her exit. I kind of found that sexy, too.

"Damn, brother, I was having grade school flashbacks." Kyle chuckled.

"All that was missing was you pulling her hair," Max threw in.

"Mark this, assholes. If we had more time, I'd be doing more than tugging on Miss Sex Kitten's curly mane. Holy hell, those legs in those sky-high heels. Hot damn. And that mouth, she can throw some sexy attitude my way anytime," I told the group.

"Keep your dick in your pants. Recon only," Declan mumbled.

"Copy that, Boss."

"Brooks wishes he had time for a quick recon mission." Thad laughed at his own joke.

We made our way out of the UN annex building, and for once I didn't feel the need to bitch about the temperature when the heat blasted me in the face. I had better things to think about, like all the ways I could fluster Tatiana Jones.

"What has you laughing?" Max asked.

"Just thinking about how pissed she's gonna be tomorrow morning when she finds out I've already been diving and cleared the area."

"You gonna tell her?" Kyle joined in.

"Hell, yeah."

"Please do not fuck this op up. In and out, that's it," Declan groaned.

"That's what he's hoping for, a quick in and out." Thad clapped Declan on the shoulder. "Don't worry, we'll still be on schedule, he only takes five minutes."

Declan cracked the smallest of smiles and shook his head. As the newcomer on our team, he'd learn we jackassed around but when it was go-time, we were on our game and as deadly as we needed to be.

CHAPTER 2

I'd given Brooks Miller too much headspace over the last twelve-plus hours. I didn't give a flying rat's ass what he and his team needed to do in Bahrain. As long as they didn't interfere with my mission objective, they could frolic in the Gulf all they wanted.

If that was the case, why the hell was I standing on the dock at slip fifteen at four-thirty in the morning instead of in bed sleeping?

Aggravation. That was why. And maybe a little curiosity. I knew the area was clean. I'd cleared it myself, not that I'd told Brooks and his team that. I'd told them more than I should've already. I knew they didn't believe my UN cover story. I didn't need them to; as long as no one on the naval base next to the fake annex I'd set up started asking questions about my presence.

"Well, well, well." Brooks' deep rumble made me shiver, even though it was already nearing ninety degrees. "I didn't have you pegged for an early riser. Yet here you are, thirty minutes earlier than necessary. And you called *me* an overachiever."

"I don't like to be late, it's rude." His long, confident strides stopped a few feet away and he openly checked me out from the shoes I was wearing all the way up to my ponytail pulled tight on top of my head. "You know what else is rude? Staring."

"You'll find there are a lot of things I do that polite company would consider rude. You'll also figure out I don't give a shit what people think. If you take offense to me verifying you're wearing proper footwear and clothing for a boat ride, that's not my problem, Doll."

Foot, meet mouth. Shit.

"Ready to go?" I asked, instead of apologizing for my incorrect snap judgement.

"I was born ready."

Yeah, I bet he was. Guys like him were all the same. They had lingo and quick answers for everything. Brooks and his silver-tongue was no different than my ex-husband. All talk. Rules to follow. Commands to bark. Work life and private life separate, never the two shall collide until they do.

"Where'd you go, Doll?"

How'd he get so close? And why the hell was he calling me 'doll'? I had a damn name, he could use it.

"Nowhere. The boat's right here."

Needing the distance more than I cared to admit, I jumped aboard the Bayliner.

"This yours?" Brooks asked.

I wanted to laugh. I lived out of a suitcase. I didn't own a home anymore, let alone a boat.

"I'm borrowing it," I answered as he came aboard the twenty-foot vessel, his arms flexing as he maneuvered his heavy dive bag.

"Legally?"

That made me smile. "This time."

"Damn, a woman after my own heart."

I didn't want to touch that statement with a ten-foot pole. So instead I started the engine. Without me having to ask, he untied the lines from the dock and neatly coiled the ropes like the good sailor he once was.

"You know how to operate this thing?"

I didn't dignify his question with a verbal answer. Instead, I pushed the throttle forward and pulled away from the dock, past the other boats, and out of the harbor.

"You don't talk much, do you?"

"I do when I've got something to say," I told him.

The crisp breeze off the Gulf and the pink-tinged horizon made me miss home. It felt like a lifetime ago since I'd been in the U.S. And I hadn't stepped foot back in San Diego since my divorce. Though I still had a storage unit there packed full of shit I didn't need and didn't want. Yet, I couldn't get myself to junk it. Memories of a past life. The end of what I thought was a dream come true but in reality, it was an epic mistake.

The spray of saltwater reminded me how much I used to love to wade out into the cold Pacific surf. Long morning swims before I headed home to an empty apartment with nothing else to do with my day until James Monroe returned home from base and started his daily bitch-fests. God, I didn't miss that part. Didn't miss how unproductive I'd been. After I stupidly quit a job I loved to start a family that would never materialize.

"Tatiana?" Brooks pulled me from wayward thoughts.

"Huh?"

"You daydream a lot."

"Just thinking about home." *Why the hell had I admitted that?* With a shake of my head I continued, "Sorry, what did you say?"

"Where's home?"

That was a good question. But an even better one was, why the hell was I thinking about San Diego in the first place? I'd long ago shoved that particular regret into a box with a big red label that read, "do not revisit—ever."

"Here. There. Wherever the UN sends me."

"Right. So we're back to the bullshit cover story."

"We've never deviated from it. And it's not bullshit. I do indeed work for the UN."

I slowed the boat and prepared to drop anchor. We were about one-hundred yards from the King Fahd Causeway Middle Island.

"The work order detailed transoceanic cabling from Middle Island to Umm an Naasan Island. The area is clear. No one has—"

"I know."

"You know?" I squinted my eyes, the narrowing of my lids had nothing to do with the fast-rising sun. "What does that mean?"

"I decided to take a dip the first day we got here and check things out. I agree with your assessment; it's clear."

"Why the fuck are we out here then, Brooks?"

"Beautiful morning for a boat ride?"

"Are you kidding me?" I seethed.

"Nope."

He strolled leisurely to the open bow and sat on the vinyl bench seat, spreading his arms before resting them on the railing. Just as smug as he could be.

"You're unbelievable. But I should've expected someone like you to pull this bullshit stunt."

"There you go again with *someone like me*. Care to expand on that, Doll?"

"No. And stop calling me *doll*."

"Would you prefer 'sweetheart'?"

He was infuriating.

"Absolutely not. I'd prefer you to not call me anything and stop wasting my time."

"You're the one who offered to take me out. As a matter of fact, you ordered me to meet you on the dock. I'm simply here at your request."

Unbelievable. Arrogant bastard.

I put the boat into gear and gave it more throttle than necessary. The engine whined, the bow raised, and I didn't hide my smile when Brooks had to grip the rails to prevent himself from falling.

His answering chuckle wasn't what I'd expected. Not that I could hear over the wind but I could see it. *Jerk.*

I slowed my speed once I approached the marina. Brooks stood and made his way back to the deck and stopped too close. I could smell his spicy scent over the briny smell of the Gulf. How had I missed that before?

"Do you have a security detail?" he weirdly asked.

"No."

"You picked up a tail."

"What?"

"Those two." He nodded in the direction of an empty slip. "They followed you here from your apartment. You know them?"

"I don't think so." Suddenly his statement clicked. "Wait. You followed me here from my apartment?"

"Stop the boat, Tatiana."

Apparently I hadn't reacted quickly enough for Brooks. His hand covered mine on the throttle and he jammed it in reverse. The Bayliner jerked into gear and he pulled back hard. The engine sputtered, Brooks turned the wheel, the boat spun left, he slammed the lever forward barely giving the engine time to disengage before he propelled us forward much like I'd done earlier.

"What the hell?"

"Reach in my back-left pocket, take out my cell."

"Why. What's—"

My question was cut off when the first bullet whizzed past us. I yanked his phone out of his pocket. He rattled off the number to dial and took the cell phone from me, placing it against his ear.

I turned back to the dock, happy to see we were gaining distance but not nearly enough. I heard him tell whoever he was speaking to that we'd found trouble. But I was more concerned at what I was seeing to pay attention to his conversation.

"Uh, Brooks? I think they have an RPG."

His head snapped over his shoulder, his cell hit the deck, and the last thing he said to me was, "I hope you can swim."

His arms wrapped around me and we jumped overboard.

Hitting the water at forty-plus knots was shocking. It was not a graceful dive into a smooth pond. I went in shoulder-first and instead of coming right up, Brooks pulled us farther under. With my arm in his tight grasp, he swam deep. My lungs burned, in desperate need of oxygen. I struggled, trying to get out of his hold. I was a decent swimmer but I wasn't prepared for a free dive to the deep-blue yonder.

He stopped his descent, pulled me face-to-face with him. Saltwater stung my eyes but I was transfixed. He was so close and looked at ease.

A shockwave sent us tumbling through the water. Brooks' relentless grip moved to my hands and didn't budge. The need to inhale overwhelmed me. Time slowed to milliseconds, as each ticked by, I fought the urge to breathe. I was suffocating.

Strong arms wrapped around my useless body and propelled us toward the surface. If I hadn't known better, I'd swear we were being thrust upward by DPV. Brooks shoved me above water and blessed air filled my lungs. A second later his head popped out of the water and he looked completely unaffected.

"You okay?"

I was heaving too hard to answer and settled for a nod.

"Roll to your back and float. It will be easier to catch your breath."

I tried and failed to do as he suggested. Finally, Brooks took pity and maneuvered me face side up. I was concentrating on the cloudless sky, counting my breaths when he spoke again. "That's it. Slow your breathing."

"What the hell?" I finally panted out.

"You ready to tell me why someone's trying to kill you?"

If I still didn't need his hands under me to help me float, I would've swam away from him. However, my lungs were still burning and my limbs wouldn't cooperate.

"Maybe *you* were the target."

"Negative."

"How do you know?"

"I haven't been in Bahrain long enough to piss anyone off. And the enemies I've made over the years wouldn't be so sloppy."

What a smug bastard. He even had to outdo me in an assassination attempt. Of course anyone who would possibly come after him would be far more sophisticated than someone trying to kill me. Yet another thing I didn't miss about my ex-husband. I couldn't even tell him I needed a jacket because I was chilly without the programmed response of: *you don't know cold until you know Navy SEAL cold.*

"Damn, you have a chip on your shoulder." He chuckled.

Who the hell laughed while treading water after being a hair's breadth away from being blown up by an RPG?

"I didn't say anything."

"You didn't have to. Your eyes say everything you don't. Hate to tell you this, Doll, but you can't hide shit."

"Were you able to tell your team where to find us?"

"Yep."

"And?"

"We wait. They'll be along shortly."

"Be along shortly? What does that mean?"

"It means just that, we wait. I can't see the dock from here. Which means I don't know if someone is waiting there for us. While I could swim back undetected, I don't think you want me leaving you out here by yourself to float. So, we wait together."

As much as it pissed me off, he was right. I could swim the almost half-mile back to the dock, but it wouldn't be any covert maneuver, that was for sure. And while he made treading water look like a walk in the park, there was no way I wanted to find out if I could do it for the length of time it would take him to go to shore and come back.

No, my best bet was to float on my back, with my mouth shut and wait for his team to come.

Fuck. I hated being the damsel in distress, but there was nothing I could do.

CHAPTER 3

"You need to relax, Doll."

Even with Tatiana's lips flattened and her brows drawn, she was a pretty woman. I wished I could smooth the worry lines on her forehead. I could've told her this was an easy day, floating out there in the warm water of the Gulf, but I didn't think she'd appreciate my comment. She didn't seem to like anything I had to say. Yesterday it'd been fun pushing her buttons, even more when we she stopped to drop anchor, but now it seemed cruel. I may've been a lot of things, but malicious wasn't one of them.

There was something working behind her intelligent eyes, and it looked a lot like pain. Not the physical kind, the emotional aftermath of heartache. It was the only thing that explained why she had the need to hide behind piss and vinegar. I wouldn't go as far as calling her a bitch, but damn she had snark. It was unfortunate for her, I liked sassy and spirited women. Her demeanor in no way was a deterrent. She was waving the proverbial red flag in front of the bull.

"And you need to stop calling me 'Doll.'"

Yeah, I liked her spunk. I wanted to call her baby cakes just to see what she'd do but I was too afraid she'd drown.

"Okay. *Tatiana*. While we're waiting, why don't we talk about your job? What does a political affairs officer do?"

If it were possible for her to become stiffer in the water, she did. "What do you want to know?"

"I want to know the real reason you're in Bahrain, but I doubt you'll tell me that. So tell me about working for the UN."

"I analyze security reports and verify information."

"How do you verify the intel you receive?"

"It depends on the region. Sometimes, I'm strapped to a platoon, normally Army. Other times I'm on my own." She turned her face from the sky and looked at me. "Aren't you getting tired?"

"No. I can do this all day."

"Of course you can. Drownproofing, phase one."

Her reference to my BUD/s training gave me pause. She'd read my file, knew I was a former SEAL, and Basic Underwater Demolition SEAL school wasn't top secret, however most people don't know the different phases. Or that there *were* different phases.

"That and I've spent a lot of time in the water. What do you know about the phases, anyway?"

She looked back to the sky and was quiet for so long, I didn't think she was going to answer. And when she did, she shocked the shit out of me.

"I was married to a SEAL. He was an instructor."

"No shit. Who?"

"James Monroe."

"Monroe? Chief Monroe from ST-1?"

"Yep. That's him."

Holy shit, that guy was a dick. And it explained so much about her attitude. He was an egomaniac and was dangerous. Monroe was infamous among team guys. During an extraction he'd refused to listen to the four-man SWCC crew, took over the special operation craft and crashed it. His stupidity had almost killed everyone on board. He was sent to BUD/s to be an instructor. The SEAL equivalent of being benched.

"So yesterday when you said you were familiar with men like me, you were comparing me to shit-for-brains Monroe?"

At least she had the decency to wince. "Not exactly him. I was generalizing. I've worked with SPECOPS guys before. You're all pretty much the same. Arrogant alpha males with big egos."

"I think you're mixing up arrogance and confidence."

"All the same."

"No, Doll. Not even close. An arrogant man will tell you how good he is. A confident one will remain silent. He doesn't need to tell you what he's capable of and most of the time, he doesn't want you to know." I'd spent years working with the best of best. Not only with the men on my team but men and women from other agencies who would prefer no one knew what their job really was. "You said *was* married. How long have you been divorced?"

"A few years."

I heard a faint whine of an engine and scanned the

area. We were sitting ducks out here in the water. There was nowhere to hide. Tatiana was finally relaxed on her back floating but I didn't think she was ready for another sixty-second trip underwater.

"If I tell you to go, you go. Swim deep and as far as you can go in one breath. When you come up, you do so slowly. Turn on your side, only take your mouth out of the water and dip back down. Do not wait for me. Do not try to help me. You leave. Understood?"

"But—"

"No buts, Doll. Understood?"

The boat was drawing near, she'd seen it, too. I had no time to explain why I needed her away from me and on her way to safety.

"Understood," she clipped, obviously not happy with my demand.

Tough shit. I couldn't do much to protect her while we were in the water. I was impressed with Tatiana. When she'd finally caught her breath, she hadn't freaked out about the boat exploding. Hadn't said a word about me tossing her overboard. It made me wonder how many times she'd been in a similar situation. She didn't even appear to be scared. Most people would be freaking out, but not Tatiana, she was a cool customer. I was going to tell her to start swimming when I finally heard the three sharp whistles I'd been waiting for.

"We're good. It's the guys."

"Don't you have to do something? Should we wave or something?"

"Nope. Just float. They'll find us."

"So. Um. Thanks for…saving me."

"That sounded painful to say. But there's no need to thank me."

"Not painful. I'm just not used to being helpless."

"There's nothing helpless about you. And you've done great."

"Sure I have. All I've done is float and you've distracted me from the fact we almost died a fiery death, then I almost drowned."

"You saved us to begin with. You're the one that saw the RPG."

Thank God, Tatiana had been looking back at the dock, or we'd have been fish food.

The boat was close enough I could make out my team on board, and weirdly I was bummed our time alone in the water had come to an end. There was something about the woman that made me want to get to know her better. Which was an impossibility since we were leaving in a few days. Shit timing.

CHAPTER 4

Once we were in the boat, the inquisition started. Declan was peppering me with questions I couldn't answer. Not because I didn't know, but I was bound by operational security. The more I tried to deflect the more frustrated he became.

"What can you tell us, Tatiana?" he asked.

"Nothing."

"Fucking hell," he grumbled. Thankfully, Kyle was piloting the boat closer to shore. The faster I got back to the annex the better. "You almost get my man killed today and you've got nothing."

"Just to point out, if he hadn't pulled his bullshit, he would've been safe and sound in his bed on base. So don't pile your shit on me. I asked all of you nicely to inspect what you need, gather your intel, and get out of Bahrain. Now I'm telling you, stay the hell away from me. I don't need to be seen with any of you, and that includes you coming into the annex."

"We came to you, at your request," Declan reminded me.

He was correct, they had. Once I'd gotten word Zane Lewis had sent a team of commandos into Bahrain, I felt it necessary to find out why they were there. When I called Tex and asked him for the meeting, I hadn't known Declan Crenshaw was the team leader. I was familiar with Declan's work while he was with the CIA. Last I'd heard, he was going deep cover, then I quit the CIA. I had no idea he'd gone to work for Zane's company, Z Corps. Maybe if I had, I wouldn't have requested a sit down. He was known around the agency as a rabid dog when he wanted intel.

"And now I'm requesting you to leave," I told Declan. "You know there is no transoceanic cabling being laid. I'm sure you're all smart enough to know the Militrix government contract is nothing more than a way to funnel money."

"What do you know about Militrix funneling money?" Brooks asked.

"Nothing."

It wasn't a bold-face lie, it was more of a small, white lie. I didn't know a lot about Militrix, however the name had come up enough in my investigation and I was now actively looking into them.

Kyle pulled into the marina and slowed. Max and Thad were both preparing to tie us off. I stood, grateful the warm sun had quickly started to dry me off.

"Whose boat is this?"

"No clue," Thad responded.

I wasn't shocked they borrowed the vessel without

permission, but I was impressed they were gently putting it back, presumably where they'd taken it from. The men went to great efforts not to allow the fiberglass boat to slam against the wooden dock.

"Well. Thanks for the pickup."

"Whoa there, Doll. You're not going anywhere until we figure out who took a shot at us."

"Were you not listening? I have work to do and being seen in public with the five of you will make that impossible."

"How do you figure that?" Brooks stood in front of me on the rocking boat with his feet planted shoulder's width, muscular arms crossed over his impressive chest, and made no move to allow me to pass.

"Seriously? It's not like the five of you don't stand out like a sore thumb around here or anything, you scream American Soldier."

"And that would be a problem for you, why?" he continued.

Now he was pissing me off. He wasn't stupid, none of them were.

"Brooks…"

"Tatiana…"

He was infuriating.

I crossed my arms. "We're not doing this out here in the open."

"Glad you see it our way. We'll discuss this when we get back to the compound."

"I'm not going anywhere with any of you. You're going to fuck everything up." I tried to keep the snarl out of my tone, but it was difficult.

I'd worked my ass off over the last few months getting everything into place. I was so close to wrapping up this op and now I had to deal with G.I. Joe and the Real American Action Hero bunch.

Brooks brushed my hair away from my face, leaned in close, and whispered, "Your options are to walk with us to the car and come quietly or I toss your little ass over my shoulder and take you there myself. I don't care how much you kick and scream."

"You wouldn't dare."

"Trust me, I would. I've had a shit morning, I want some dry clothes and a cup of coffee."

"That's it? Dry clothes and coffee?"

"Coffee then business. So what will it be, Doll? Option one or two?"

"I will kick you in the balls if you try to put me over your shoulder."

"Then I hope for the sake of my future children you choose the first option."

He was serious. And he knew that it wouldn't matter how loudly I screamed and fought. No one would come to my aid. He also knew I'd never draw attention to myself, or them, by kicking and yelling.

Bastard.

"You have one hour, then I have work I need to do."

Kyle, Thad, and Max were already waiting on the dock. Brooks moved to the side and offered his hand to help me climb off the boat. I declined. We'd done enough touching for one day. The rumble of his laugh made my female parts wake up and take notice, only proving I'd done the right thing by not placing my hand in his. He was an unwelcome distraction. I had to stay focused, not only did I have others depending on me, but I wanted out of Bahrain alive. I didn't have time to play games with the good-looking mercenary. Even if he was sexy as sin and it had been a long time since I'd had the pleasure of a man's company.

"I'd love to know where you go when you drift off." Brooks' hot breath fanned over my neck. I pulled back and my gaze snapped to his. Mirth danced across his face.

With his hair tousled and that smile, he looked a step down from deadly. But when my eyes looked at his wet t-shirt clinging to his well-defined chest, I remembered. He was no different than who he was, a lethal mercenary with the ego to go with the job title.

"My head is a boring place."

"There's not a boring thing about you."

Off limits, I reminded myself as we walked to the car. His smooth talk, hard body, and suggestive smile were one hundred percent off limits.

* * *

I'd stupidly been lost in thought while Declan drove. It took me a moment to take in my surroundings and figure out we were still about thirty minutes away from the base.

Declan pulled in front of an unfamiliar gated compound. "Where are we?"

Max exited the car and Brooks answered, "A safe house."

"I thought you were staying at the naval base."

"We have a room there," he answered, but didn't elaborate further.

Max had the gate opened, bringing into view a simple two-story U-shaped structure. Declan pulled into the courtyard and Max shut the gate, closing us off from the street. The walls around the compound were much taller than the normal eight-to-ten-foot barricades around the homes in the area. The outside of the house was well-kept, there was nothing exceptional or noteworthy other than the added perimeter security.

The six of us walked through an unlocked door and the interior was practically empty. There were two couches in what would be considered the main living area but no other furniture or decoration. When I followed Declan into the dining room, I was surprised to find a large table and modern kitchen off to the side.

Kyle, Max, and Thad had disappeared leaving me alone with Brooks and Declan.

"Where'd everyone go?"

"Kyle and Max will take post on the second floor and Thad's going to the safe," Declan answered.

"Are you expecting an invasion?"

"No. But we weren't expecting an assassination attempt this morning, either."

"Touché."

"Do you have any idea who would want to kill you?" Declan started.

"Boy, you don't waste time, do you? Brooks and I are still wet from our little swim and you're just diving right in."

Okay, I was stalling. It was nearing a hundred degrees

and my shorts and t-shirt were mostly dry already. Brooks had to be uncomfortable in his damp cargo pants and… when had he taken off his boots? And why was I staring at the man's bare feet?

Thad came back in the room and set a Sig P226 on the table in front of Brooks. He simply nodded his thanks, dropped the magazine, checked it was loaded, slammed the mag back into place, and tucked it into the back of his cargo pants.

"Tatiana," Declan snapped.

Shit. So much for trying to delay. I had to give them something. "Not everyone in the region is happy I'm here. My last report outlined the instability in the area."

The last part of my statement was a complete fabrication. I hadn't turned in any reports.

"Bullshit," Thad spoke. "A report about Bahrain's volatility isn't something new. You said you had something going down in a week. What do you have planned?"

"Need to know," I answered.

"We're in the need," Declan said.

"You're not even in the ballpark, Declan. I understand why your team is here. You have an objective. I have no doubt you can complete your mission and head out."

"Doll, someone tried to kill me today—"

"No. They tried to kill *me*. You had the unfortunate luck of being with me. And I will point out again if you hadn't pulled that stupid stunt this morning, you wouldn't have been."

"Are we seriously going to stand around and split hairs about who was the target?"

"There's no splitting anything. You've already pointed

out anyone making an attempt on your life wouldn't have been so careless. We all know I was the intended target. End of story. I'm not at liberty to tell you why I'm here. I'd appreciate the respect of you not asking again. Now since we're at an impasse, if someone will take me back to the dock, I'd like to go home. I have work to do."

"And how do you plan on getting home from the dock? I'm sure your keys are on the bottom of the Gulf." Brooks smirked.

Ass.

I shoved my hand in my pocket, unclipped my car key from the safety pin, and held it out for him to see.

Before I could wipe his nose in the fact I wasn't a rookie, Thad cut in. "We have company."

"Feel like talking yet?" Declan asked again.

"Nope. But the sooner I'm away from you five the faster you'll be able to complete your recon without people shooting at you."

"This happen to you often?" he continued.

"Typically not twice in one day."

That was the sad reality of my life. I spent the majority of it dodging bullets. Scumbags didn't like it when I shut their rackets down and stopped the flow of money. It was simple economics.

"Five armed males. There are two in the cab of the truck, three in the bed," Thad reported.

Declan pulled his phone out of his pocket, swiped the screen, and walked out of the room.

"Not twice a day, huh? Is it safe to say you're taking fire once a day, then?" Brooks asked.

"No. Not every day. I really need to get back to work."

I couldn't decipher the strange look on his face. His jaw ticked and his eyes narrowed. I was happy Declan had returned, until he spoke.

"No reason for you to rush off now," Declan said. "The annex is on fire."

"What the fuck? I have to go."

"You have orders to stay put."

I took a moment to stare at the ceiling and blow out a calming breath. Declan was full of shit. I didn't have orders to do anything.

"We're done playing games, Declan. I've shown you and your team nothing but respect and now you're lying to me. I'm leaving."

Brooks stepped in front of me halting my exit. "I'm not fucking around, Brooks."

Thad broke into our standoff. "Three hostiles are out of the bed of the pickup, patrolling the front gate."

I was screwed. Five men were going to break through the gate any second and when they did, I needed to be armed.

CHAPTER 5

Tatiana's eyes held mine before they shifted to Declan.

"The men outside work for a man named, Matek Nazari. They've been hired to kill me—"

"Who is he?" Declan cut her off.

"A trafficker—"

"Human?" he asked.

"Any minute they're going to breach the gate," Tatiana snarled. "This would go a lot faster if you'd let me finish without interruptions. He traffics ancient artifacts. I was posing as a competing buyer. I put in a bid Nazari wasn't happy with. He's been sending his men after me to try and take out the competition. Things were going as planned until you guys showed up. I was letting them play their games. Unfortunately for them, now I have to take them out. I can't risk them going back to Nazari and reporting I've been seen with American soldiers."

"You're agency?" I couldn't hide my distaste. "Not that any of us were buying the UNPOA cover."

"I'm…something. Which is not up for discussion. What else do you have in the weapons cache?" She directed her question to Declan.

My team leader eyed her before he turned to Thad, and with a lift of his chin Thad jogged out of the room.

"What do you know about the guys out front?"

"Nothing. The only thing I know is they miss. Before today, they've made three attempts, all as sloppy as the current situation. Nazari is a heavy hitter but apparently hires his hits out on the cheap."

Thad came back in the room with two HK416 rifles. He handed one to Tatiana before passing one to me. Next he pulled fully loaded magazines from the pockets of his cargo pants. Finally, he passed her a Sig P226, identical to the 9mm pistol he'd handed me earlier.

I don't know what kind of man it made me, but watching her inspect the rifle she'd been given was turning me on. She fingered the mag release button, ejected it, confirming it was loaded, jammed it back into place, and pulled back on the charging handle. The sound of the metal slamming, pushing a bullet into the chamber, was some sort of tactical foreplay I'd never experienced.

"Two tangos broke south," Thad informed us. "They're moving around back."

"You two, take the back. Thad, you're with me out front," Declan told us, then repeated his instructions into a two-way radio adding, "Max, Kyle, you stay on the second floor."

Tatiana picked up two of the extra .223 magazines and shoved them in the back pocket of her shorts like some sexy *Guns & Ammo* calendar girl, further making my lust grow. What the fuck was wrong with me? This was a first, never had I had a hard-on going into a gun fight.

"Ready?" I asked.

With a nod, she followed me down a hallway and out the back door. The waist-high wall surrounding the cement patio was the perfect place to take cover while we waited to see if these assholes could breach the outer perimeter.

"What's your guess? Do you think they'll try and come over or blow their way through?" I asked.

Not that it mattered which way they tried to break in, they'd be dead before they were two feet onto the property. The only difference it would make was, where the mess would be left to clean up.

Tatiana looked around the back courtyard before she answered. "They won't try and breach back here. The second their heads poke over the wall they'll be popped. No one's that stupid. And I don't think they have the explosive charges to blast in."

Just as she finished her statement, a head came up over the wall. Without giving away our hiding spot, I raised my rifle and pulled the trigger. The man disappeared from sight.

"You were saying?"

"I'm beginning to feel a little cheated. Nazari sent the B-Squad of hitmen to kill me. He didn't think I was worthy of an experienced team."

Two quick gunshots came from out front, followed by a rapid fire. Not moving was one of the hardest instincts I had to break the first time I was deployed. The natural need to rush to your team's back when they were taking fire instead of holding the position you were ordered.

"Desperation to finish a job makes people sloppy," I told her, still scanning the area for the other man.

Three sharp whistles cut through the now silent morning. "We're clear."

"Well, that was no fun," Tatiana complained.

Her declaration had my dick jerking in my cargos. Why did I find her thirst for enemy blood so arousing? She wasn't the first woman I'd seen with a gun, nor the first in combat. But there was something different about her. The first time I'd met Tatiana she was in a skirt and a pair of heels that made me want to fall to my knees and give thanks to whoever had designed the sexy shoes. Right before I found a flat surface to lie her on to worship every inch of her. She had been proper and mostly bitchy. A far cry from the woman I'd been stranded in the water with.

But this version of her, the strong, capable gun handler in a pair of shorts and soggy sneakers… off-the-charts-erotic as fuck. All that was missing was her throwing her spunky attitude my way and I'd be a love-sick fool.

With another quick look around, I stood, and Tatiana followed my lead. Once we were back into the safety of the house, I stopped blocking her progression and backed her against the plaster wall. Uncaring there was a fully-automatic weapon between us, I leaned in close.

"Who are you, Doll?"

"No one special."

"Now that right there is the biggest crock of shit you've tried to feed me. Who are you, Tatiana Jones?"

"A ghost. A no one. A loner with no friends, no team, no home address." Her words were strong but her expression was sad. "No different than you."

She was incorrect, we weren't the same. I had my team and I couldn't imagine them not having my back. It made all the long, hard missions easier. Each of us had given up a part of who we were to continue to serve our country. But my closest friends were always with me.

"The phone's for you, Tatiana," Declan said, ending my time alone with her. "Brooks, help us drag the bodies into the courtyard."

I stepped back allowing her to move around me and take the phone from Dec. It was the wrong time and the wrong place for me to have to adjust my hard-on in an effort to hide it, but there I was with my hand on my crotch.

"I now understand why Zane is always complaining," Declan grouched as we walked out the front door.

"Why's that?"

"Trying to keep a team of assholes in line and their dicks in their pants would make anyone grumpy."

"My dick never left my pants."

"And it's a good thing. That woman is not who she says she is."

"No shit."

Declan stopped at the gate and turned to face me. "No, Brooks. She's not who any of us thought she was. She's not agency."

"Who is she?"

"You two gonna help before the defense force shows

up or stand around and gossip?" Kyle asked as he dragged a body into the courtyard.

Without another word, Declan jogged off, leaving me wondering who the fuck Tatiana Jones really was and who she worked for. I didn't pull out of my stupor until Kyle passed me on his way back to the street and slapped me on the back.

"Come on, lover boy, we got stiffs to stack."

It took us less than ten minutes to move the bodies and shut the gate behind us. Zane had arranged for a clean-up crew to come in and dispose of the men. No one had IDs or any marks that would help us figure out their identities. We'd have to wait until our intel specialist back in Maryland ran the fingerprints Declan had scanned and emailed.

The moment we entered the house I knew she was gone. I didn't need to see Dec's cell phone and the HK416 lying on the table to know. Interestingly enough, she hadn't left the Sig P226. For some reason, that made me smile. Sneaky bitch ran off with one of our handguns. It was all the reason I needed to track her down. I couldn't have her stealing company property.

"She left you a note." Dec handed me a slip of paper.

Brooks,

Thanks for today.

I owe you one.

T.

"Who was she talking to?"

"Don't know. Her handler if I had to guess. He knew the color and mission code so I let him speak to her."

Who the fuck was Tatiana and where did she go?

CHAPTER 6

It had been two days since I'd seen Tatiana and there was a knot in my gut the size of a boulder. We'd gone by what was left of the fire-bombed annex but there was nothing there. We'd checked her apartment, the one I'd followed her from the morning of our ill-fated boat ride, and it was empty.

"Brooks! Get in here," Declan called from the dining room.

Max, Thad, and Kyle were already around the table waiting for me.

"What's up?"

"Rocco, Ace, and Gumby are MIA."

Yesterday when we were at the naval base talking to the MPs about the fire at the annex we were shocked to run into Gumby and Ace outside of the temporary tenant quarters. The three men were a part of a six-man SEAL team stationed in San Diego. We'd actually worked a recovery mission with them not too long ago. An international group of the power elite known as The Omni had made the mistake of initiating a bad play. They'd taken down Marine One and had kidnapped the president. The only thing the group had done was piss off Tom Anderson, and expose where his security weaknesses were. Those holes had not only been patched but double fortified. The Omni Group had been on every US three-letter-agency radar for years. The issue had always been their membership was a closely guarded secret. Not even the impressive John "Tex" Keegan could break their code. That was until recently. Now we knew, Omni members held positions of power in our government. What that meant exactly was anyone's guess.

"Come again?"

"Tex called. They missed their last check-in. It's been over twenty-four hours," Dec reaffirmed.

"Last known coordinates?" I asked.

"Need to know."

"Hate to state the obvious," Thad began, "but we need to know.'

Thad was our team's *MacGyver*. There was nothing the man couldn't hot wire, fix, or rig. Unfortunately, none of his impressive skills would help us track the three men.

"Tex is working on it. So far, it's a no-go. Grab your shit, we're out of here in five."

"Copy that," Max agreed and double-timed it out of the room with Kyle hot on his heels.

"Any idea where to start?"

Ace and Gumby had said they were in Bahrain on a special assignment, but hadn't elaborated. Other than us knowing they were staying on base and some woman had caught Rocco's eye, we were flying blind. Hell, they hadn't even told us the woman's name that Rocco had the hots for.

"Manama seems like a good place."

Manama was not a good place, it was a hotbed of criminal activity. A slum that you didn't want to be in after dark. But it was the perfect place for a Navy SEAL to go hunting.

Max and Kyle came back with their kit, reminding me I needed to go grab my go-bag. I made my way to the bedroom I'd been staying in and glanced around the small space. Not the worst accommodations, not even in the bottom hundred shittastic places I'd had to bed down over the last ten years.

Sometimes it was easier sleeping out in the desert under the stars, with distant gunfire and bombs to lull me to sleep. Hotel rooms, military quarters, and temporary compounds were a tease. Just enough comfort to make you miss home. Wherever home was. I didn't have one of those anymore. Uncle Sam had provided everything I'd needed to survive for eight years and Zane Lewis had kept me moving for the last two. I didn't own a damn thing; I was as free as the wind. I had a bank account I rarely touched and my passport, albeit an alias, was stamped full. We'd been back to the states three times in the last few years.

We were supposed to be INCONUS for sixty-days of R and R. I'd planned on going off grid and finding a place to be alone. Now all I could think about was what it would be like to have a few days of down time with the elusive Tatiana. Alone didn't sound all that appealing anymore. Not when I couldn't stop thinking about the beautiful woman's smile. Not to mention, the way she'd handled her gun, reminding me of a way sexier upgrade of Sarah Connor. Days later, I still couldn't purge her from my thoughts. It was driving me crazy not knowing where she was or who exactly she worked for.

"Two minutes." Dec's voice pulled me from my thoughts.

* * *

"You got eyes on the woman in the black and pink abaya?" I quietly asked. "Two o'clock. Just got out of a taxi."

"Roger." Declan came back through my earpiece.

It was after eleven at night, we were smack dab in the middle of a red zone. An area the US embassy and common sense would tell you to stay the fuck away from. It was out of the touristy section of the city. The streets were dirty, building and shops dilapidated, the stench of poverty thick in the air. It was mere miles from the heart of opulence and wealth, but it might as well have been a whole other country. The Crowne Plaza Bahrain this place was not.

A woman walking by herself stood out. A woman who was struggling to walk in the long abaya that looked to be brand new might as well have had a flashing strobe over her saying, *violate me.* Women were not supposed to be out by themselves without a male accompanying them. Unless of course they were a *woman of the night* working a street corner. Which this woman clearly was not.

"Is she crazy? She's gonna get herself killed out here," Max added.

"What are you thinking?" Declan asked.

Bahrain was our first official mission with Declan at the helm. So far, he was proving to be a good leader. During the planning of the operation he'd asked us our thoughts and how we would run the op. Once he'd had all of our input, he'd adjusted his initial plan. Not all of it, but he'd seen the value in other's perspectives.

"The abaya is new. Too expensive for this area. She can barely walk in it. She's adjusted her hijab several times. Her head is on a swivel. There's no way she belongs here, and I doubt she's ever worn a head covering, or the long robe."

"Agreed," Dec said.

"What's your gut telling you, Brooks?"

"We follow her."

"Stay spread out. Do not engage," he reminded us.

We were all armed to the teeth. Though none of us needed to draw a weapon to neutralize a threat, we'd never be in this neighborhood of Manama unarmed.

Sweat was pouring down my back under my heavy body armor. Even this late in the evening it was hotter than Hades. What I wouldn't give for a cold brew and a nice cool breeze.

"What the hell is she doing?" Max asked.

We'd followed the woman almost a mile into an alleyway behind a grocery store.

I couldn't see him, I couldn't see any of my teammates through the darkness, they blended into the shadows like the ghosts we were. I flipped down my night vision goggles. With everything tinted green, I watched the woman push a box under a window and hoist herself through.

"Is she robbing a grocery store?" Max inquired, as the woman slipped through the small space.

A grocery store in this area was a loose term. The shops in Manama would sell everything from near rotting food to a variety of household items.

"Doubt it," I answered.

Call it a gut feeling or hard-won intuition. There was zero chance she was simply out for a stroll this late at night to rob a store this far into the heart of a shithole. Her clean abaya was another tell, she wasn't a street rat scrounging for her next meal. And she was too clumsy to be a professional.

"We'll give it five minutes," Declan instructed.

"Roger."

I held my position at the back entrance, not bothering to take my eyes off the door. I knew my team had the building surrounded and would call in if there were unfriendlies in the vicinity.

"She's moving something and not trying to be quiet about it," Max informed us. A few minutes later he came back with, "Something's definitely going on in there. I don't know if the owner of the store caught her, but there's a scuffle for sure."

"Hold your positions. B and E is not our concern," Declan reminded us.

I hated this shit. There was something inherently wrong knowing a woman was most likely being hurt but not being able to do a damn thing about it. Rules of engagement and culture prevented us from intervening. We had our mission, saving a woman from the punishment she'd face for stealing was not it.

"Someone is exiting the back window. Male." I was too far away to make out features but there was no mistaking it was a man. "Male number two is out. The woman. And a third male," I called in.

"Hold fast," came from Declan.

I looked through my spotting scope, zooming in until I had a clear picture of the men's faces. "Rocco, Ace, Gumby, and the unidentified female."

"Injuries?" Dec asked.

"They've been beat to hell, but I don't see any GSWs."

The four made their way through the alley, heading to the street. Max called in their location. "Rocco and the female broke away. Gumby and Ace are falling into the shadows."

"Max, Kyle, and Thad, follow Rocco. Do not approach. Brooks, you're with me."

I quickly got to my feet and jogged down the small embankment I'd taken cover on. I met up with Declan and we went in the direction he'd last seen Gumby and Ace.

"Whoa." My hands came up as I felt the cool blade against my throat. "It's Country." I used my call sign instead of my name.

I wasn't sure which one was behind me, but I knew it was Gumby or Ace. Sometimes it's easier to let your target come to you. Especially when dealing with men who were as highly trained in evasion as they were.

"What the hell?" Ace said, lowering his knife. "How'd you find us?"

"Tex called and said you three had gotten yourselves into a jam."

Declan and Gumby both came out of the shadows and joined us.

"You ready to get the fuck outta here, before we attract anymore attention?" Declan asked.

We kept a good distance between us and Rocco. His arm was wrapped protectively around the woman as he kept a fast clip.

"Who is that?"

"Caite McCallan," Ace answered as he took two of the four boxes Gumby was carrying.

"You want me to take those?" I asked Gumby, noticing his limp.

"I'm good," he returned, adjusting the heavy load.

"You guys get what you came for?" Declan inquired as he continually scanned the area.

"Not everything. But hopefully the commander will be happy with the new intel." Gumby tried to hide the pain as he spoke.

"What the hell happened?"

Ace gave us the abbreviated version of the last twenty-four hours, including how a mob of men had ambushed them and locked them in a cellar. How they found some ancient artifacts. And ending with a crazy woman, albeit brave, coming to their aid. Hearing what Caite had done for Rocco, Ace, and Gumby made me think about Tatiana. I wondered if my team had gone missing if she'd come searching for us. I doubted it. She had her mission and had made it painfully obvious she wanted nothing do to with any of us, me especially.

"Wait. Did you say ancient artifacts?" I interrupted Ace.

"Yeah. Some sort of tablets."

"Did Tatiana say what she was bidding on?" I asked Declan.

"Not to me."

"Who's Tatiana?" Gumby slowed his pace and watched as Rocco stepped in front of a taxi, forcing the driver to stop.

A few seconds later, both Rocco and the woman were in the car and it sped away.

"Tatiana is…" I wasn't sure how to explain her.

"Is the woman that is going to put Brooks' dick in a vise if he doesn't leave her alone," Declan helpfully supplied.

I was going to say sexy, beautiful, and smart but I was glad Dec had cut me off.

"Grab that taxi, would you?" Ace motioned toward a car coming our way. "Twenty-four hours in that cellar, I'm ready to get the hell out of here."

"Copy that."

CHAPTER 7

The Bitoo brothers were not at the store and my contact told me they hadn't checked in with Nazari. If they'd taken the tablets and run, they were screwed. Or better yet, if they'd sold them outside of the auction, they'd wish for death. There were a lot of interested buyers. So far, I was still the highest bidder on the ten Iraqi cuneiform tablets. They'd bring in a hefty price, and I'd be able to follow the money back to whichever terrorist organization was smuggling artifacts out of Bahrain.

I'd like to say my motivation was preserving the cultural and spiritual relics but it was purely about the money. It was my job to track, then intercept, payments before they could be used to buy guns and fund extremist groups hellbent on killing.

I just needed a few more days and I'd be in possession of the tablets and on my way to Iraq. Three clay cones dating back to 2,200 B.C. that had been looted after the fall of Saddam Hussein had come up for bid.

The asking price was five-million but they'd bring in closer to thirty after collectors from around the world frantically tried to get the pieces into their private exhibitions.

A knock had me looking at the villa door. No one knew I was here. I'd moved every day since the annex was firebombed and I hadn't even checked in with my handler. It was probably one of the other tenants in the building. This was one of the nicer areas of Bahrain, a small group of man-made islands. Amwaj offered the most beautiful panoramic views of the sea and was popular among expats.

Another knock pulled me from my thoughts. Checking my Sig P226 was loaded, I smiled, wondering how pissed Brooks had been when he'd come back after cleaning up dead bodies and found I wasn't there. I hadn't needed to take the Sig that belonged to them, I'd done it because… well, I wasn't sure why I took the gun. Just that I liked having something that belonged to him. Which was absolutely absurd. It wasn't like I'd ever see…

My thought was cut off when I opened the door. "Hey there, Doll."

"What are you doing here?"

"Nice to see you, too." He shouldered his way in and shut the door behind him.

"No, really, Brooks, what are you doing here?"

I didn't need anything screwing up the next few days. Brooks being here meant his team was, too. I'd gone to great lengths to make sure I wasn't being followed. Them being anywhere near me didn't mean good things. For one, I hadn't been as careful as I'd thought.

"Thought you could use some intel on the Bitoo brothers.'

"Who?" I tried to keep my face impassive even though my insides were a riot of nerves.

How in the hell did he know that name?

"Cut the shit, Tatiana. This will go much smoother if you stop playing stupid."

I didn't appreciate being called stupid, and had no issue telling him so.

"I'm far from stupid, asshole."

"I know you are, Doll. What you seem to forget is, I'm far from stupid as well. Time to stop bullshitting and lay the cards on the table."

"What cards?"

Now I was playing stupid just to piss him off. I knew what he meant, but I still wasn't ready to give him anything.

"I know you're tracking some tablets. Ten to be exact. Bad news for you is, six are in the hands of the US government. Four are unaccounted for."

"How do you know that?"

"Not at liberty to say."

"Bullshit."

"Bullshit nothing. I saw six with my very own eyes."

"Goddammit. Please tell me you're fucking with me."

If he was telling the truth, months of hard work were in the toilet.

"'Fraid not. But the good news is, we've tracked down the brothers. Consider this an olive branch."

"Olive branch?"

"Yeah, you know a gesture of goodwill."

"I know what an olive branch is. What I don't understand is why you'd want to extend one to me."

"We didn't get off on the right foot. I'd like to rectify that. Thought you'd like to go with us."

"Thanks for the offer, but I work alone."

"Suit yourself."

Brooks started for the door and my stomach dropped. I thought he'd argue his point, let me negotiate an exchange of information.

"Wait. That's it?"

"Yeah, Doll. That's it. I'm not going to force you to go with us if you're not interested. I thought you'd want in on the op. I was wrong."

"I want the intel," I told him. "How about I give you what I've found on Militrix and you give me the location of the Bitoo brothers?"

"No dice."

"Why not? It's a good deal. You're not interested in the tablets and you need the information I have on Militrix."

"It may be a good deal, but I'm not taking it. No way am I letting you try to take down five men on your own."

That pissed me off. His words were too close to the shit my ex-husband used to shovel at me. I'd worked my ass off to prove myself in this business. And it was no easy feat, I'll be dammed if I stood there and listened to Brooks and his alpha male bullshit.

"Why's that, Brooks? Because I'm a woman?"

For some unknown reason his face turned hard and the cold stare he leveled me with made me shiver. "You shittin' me? I have to say, it pisses me off you'd try that fucked-up nonsense on me. I had no problem you taking my back at the compound. Never said shit about you being a woman and staying behind in the safety of the house." He was right, he didn't, none of them did. Thad had simply handed me a rifle and sidearm and never asked if I knew how to operate either. "They're dangerous and unpredictable. They know they fucked up and lost six tablets. They also know they're as good as dead. If not by the hands of the people they've double-crossed, by the hands of the three SEALs they unsuccessfully tried to kill. Lucky for the brothers, the three men they'd locked in a cellar are alive and well and on their way back to the states. Unlucky for them, they're about to be on the receiving end of retribution. We thought you'd like to question them about the tablets before they're disposed of."

"Fuck."

"Your choice, Doll. But what isn't, is going in alone. Not a chance in hell I'll let that happen. And it has nothing to do with you being a woman, and everything to do with wanting you breathing."

I needed to find the other tablets and I couldn't do that if Brooks and his team killed them before I had a chance to talk with them.

"I want in."

"Grab your shit and let's go."

"My shit?"

"Yeah, Tatiana. Your shit. Personal belongings."

"Why? All I need is this." I pulled the Sig P226 from the waistband of my shorts and smiled when his lips twitched.

"You're with us at the compound until this is over."

"Why?" Damn, I sounded like a broken record.

"It's safer there. Time's wasting. You wanna hurry? We have an op to plan."

I weighed my options and figured it would take more energy than it was worth to argue with Brooks. Besides, even if I agreed now, it didn't mean I had to stay at the compound later. I could leave anytime I wanted. And we did need to work out a way to keep at least one of the men alive long enough for me to question.

"Give me a minute."

I rushed into the bedroom and quickly changed my clothes. I may wear shorts in the privacy of my apartment or in the early morning hours while I knew I was going on a boat. But being in a country that frowned upon women exposing any skin, I was respectful. I yanked on a pair of pants and a long-sleeved tee knowing I would be sweating through the cotton within seconds and hoping we'd be at the compound fast so I could change back.

I didn't miss Brooks' long sweeping appraisal when I walked back into the living room with my backpack over my shoulder. I didn't have time to contemplate why I liked his eyes on me, or why my insides had warmed when he had me pressed against the wall the other day. It should've pissed me off he had the audacity to invade my space, but it hadn't. I grabbed my laptop case and checked my files were secure before I joined him near the door.

"Want me to take anything?"

I felt my eyes narrowing.

"Jesus, woman, you need to relax. Everything I say isn't a slight. I was simply offering to help."

He was right, I was overreacting. “No. Thank you, I’ve got it.”

We made our way to a ratty-assed Toyota SUV that had more rust than paint left. Kyle was behind the wheel and Max was in the passenger seat. They said their hellos but other than that the drive to the compound was done in near-silence.

Once we’d entered the gated compound Max and Kyle exited the SUV, leaving me alone with Brooks.

“Everything okay?” he asked.

“Yeah, why?”

“You seem…off.”

I was beginning to learn nothing slipped Brooks’ notice. I found the observation disconcerting. I didn’t like how he could so easily read me.

“Just thinking what all of this means for my mission.”

“Let’s get inside and you out of these clothes and we’ll talk it out.”

My cheeks heated at his innocent comment. I knew what he meant, I was sweating like a pig, but I couldn’t help thinking what it would be like if he helped me out of my sweat-drenched tee. Not the sexiest thought, but an inappropriate one nonetheless.

Brooks’ eyes stayed glued to mine when he said, “I’d love to know what just ran through your mind that pinkened your pretty cheeks.”

His hand slowly came to my face, giving me every opportunity to back away or stop him, which stupidly I didn’t. I remained still even as his thumb brushed my cheek while his fingers dug into the back of my neck.

"There's something about you, Tatiana Jones, that drives me wild."

Right back atcha, Brooks Miller, was what I was thinking but didn't dare say. I hadn't been able to get him out of my mind. He'd invaded my every thought. Not good, not good at all. I had to concentrate on my mission, not on his crazy-cool hazel eyes with specks of blue. Or his too-long shaggy brown hair, or the days-old stubble on his face that would feel oh-so-good scraping my inner thighs. And I really should not have been wondering what he looked like under his tight tee and cargos.

"Good God, Doll. When you get lost in your head and your eyes go soft, right before they get heavy..." He shook his head before he continued, "That look. It can make a man weak. Make him believe in all sorts of shit. Make him want to do anything to keep it."

Weirdly, that may've been the best compliment I'd ever received. Men like Brooks were a lot of things, weak wasn't one of them.

"We can't go there, Brooks."

"Go where, Tatiana?" He smiled.

"Wherever it is this thing between us leads."

"So you admit there's something."

"I admit—" A sharp whistle had me looking out the front windshield. Thank God for the interruption. "We should go inside."

"We're not done with this conversation."

"We are. We both have an op to complete. Neither of us need the complication."

"Nothing complicated about it."

Of course he would think that. To him it would be an

exchange of bodily fluids. A way to blow off steam and get off. I hadn't been with a man since my ex-husband. Not that I'd tell him that. But undoubtedly things would get complicated.

"Not interested, Brooks."

That was a big fat lie and I knew he knew. I didn't need his words to confirm it.

He leaned in and brushed my hair off my shoulder. "Liar," he whispered against my ear. My body shivered despite the oppressive heat. "I know you feel it, too, Doll."

Asshole.

CHAPTER 8

I was crossing lines I'd promised myself I wouldn't. It was easy to take a vow of chastity when Tatiana wasn't in front of me. It was a whole other thing when I was face-to-face with her. She was correct about one thing, despite me telling her otherwise, giving in would complicate things. She was also correct when she said we both had a mission to complete. Ours was supposed to have been completed by now, taking us far from Bahrain and her. But after the tangle Rocco and the guys had found themselves in, Tex had found a connection between the tablets and Omni. Lucky for me that meant Zane had given us the go-ahead to track down Tatiana. Now I was thinking it wasn't so lucky after all. I hadn't been in her company an hour and already I was reneging on my resolution not to touch her.

"Mind if I change real quick?" she asked the second she'd walked into the house.

I was trying. Really fucking trying not to picture her nude but failing miserably.

"Use my room. First door on the right. You can leave your stuff in there. There's only five bedrooms. You can take mine." Her brow quirked up and I added, "I'll take the couch."

Thad already had a map of Bahrain spread out on the table with several other maps of the exact location of the waterfront property where the Bitoo brothers were holed up. Declan had already marked up the points of entry and exit strategy. It was a good plan.

Tatiana came back into the room and I couldn't stop myself from appreciating her long, toned legs. Christ. It was like they were tailor-made to wrap around my waist. This woman turned me into someone I wasn't proud of, an uncivilized caveman. Next, I would be beating my chest and dragging her off to my cave begging her to let me worship her. I needed my head examined—quick, fast, and in a hurry.

She placed her laptop and file folder on the table and studied the maps in front of her.

"Who owns this property?" she asked.

"It's registered to Falcon Holdings," Declan told her.

"So you found the connection between Militrix and Falcon?" Tatiana opened the file she'd set on top of her closed laptop.

"How did you find the connection? And no more lying, Doll."

She sighed and scrubbed her hands over her face before they went to her hair. She used the band on her wrist to fasten a ponytail. With her hair pulled up off her face she looked younger than her thirty-two.

"Purely by accident. I'm tracking an antiquities broker, Lucre. They're behind some of the rarest, stolen middle eastern artifacts. Lucre warehouses are owned by Falcon. I looked further and Falcon owns and manages properties all over Africa and the Middle East. I dug a little deeper into Falcon and found they're also a holding company. They own a buttload of stock in Militrix as well as several other ginormous companies." She stopped and pinned me with her dark eyes. "Your turn. How'd you find me?"

"Tex."

"Fuckin' Keegan. I should've known. So, he tracked the Bitoo brothers, too."

"No. That was all me, Doll. After they figured out the guys had escaped and took the tablets they'd hidden in the cellar, the four younger brothers went on a bender. Timothee, the eldest, had one helluva time getting his drunk brothers to shut their mouths. Bitching and complaining about the Americans. I followed them back to their hideout."

"Just like that?" She looked like she didn't believe me.

Good old fashion leg work, keep it simple and stupid. The brothers were mostly drunks. Their father had tried unsuccessfully to help them find jobs. However, they'd rather take the fast, easy illegal money than put in a hard day's work. Unfortunately, they were going to learn the hard way there were repercussions for their actions.

"Yep. Just like that."

"What's the plan?"

Declan ran down the mission specifics, outlining what

Tatiana's role was, and surprisingly she hadn't argued. Max, Thad, and Declan would be point going in first. Kyle would cover the team, and she and I would enter after the team cleared the building.

"I need at least one of them alive," she told Declan, then added, "and if they have the four tablets, I'd like those, too.'

"That's the plan," he reminded her. "But if those tablets are as valuable as Tex says they are, I would expect they're not going to give up easily."

"They are," she confirmed. "Even if only four are left, they'll bring in a good price."

"Where's the money track back to?" Kyle surprisingly asked.

We knew the answer, so either he was testing her candor or he wanted to know what she knew.

"The seller is the Lucre group. I already told you."

"Right," Kyle mumbled.

Her eyes narrowed on him. "Apparently, you didn't like my answer. So, what are you asking exactly? Do I know what Lucre does with the money? Yes, I do. They fund different terrorist organizations. Presumably to keep discord in different tribal areas of Africa. It's easier to pillage and smuggle artifacts when there is conflict among tribes."

"Are you familiar with Omni?" I inquired.

"Yes, I know the name. There's been conspiracy theories about the group for years. Why?"

"Not so much theories, Doll. The man behind Lucre, Prince Mohammad Al Issa, is indeed a member of Omni," I told her.

There was a flash of anger before she schooled her features and smirked. "So you weren't really here to check the transoceanic cabling contract?"

"We were. But in conjunction with Omni," Declan informed her. "It seems your tablets are a better lead."

"What?" Her hand went to her hip and her posture stiffened. "Now you think you're going to take over my op?"

"Not necessarily. We're offering you a…partnership. We can all work together," Dec continued.

"No fucking way. I've worked too damn hard for you guys to come in now and take over. I have my orders and I fully intend to deliver. I already told Brooks, I work alone."

She was a stubborn little thing, there was no reason for her to turn our offer down. "We don't want the tablets. Or at least not the way you're thinking. Our only goal is to take down Al Issa."

"Which fucks me."

"How so?" Kyle asked.

"I need him in business. I already told you Lucre is one of the largest smuggling operations. They sell. I buy. Then I can track whatever terrorist organization they're funding, pass my intel off, and the group is shut down or monitored. If Al Issa is taken out, Lucre crumbles. And, I'm fucked."

"Dismantling Omni is more important," Declan argued.

"Says who? You?"

Declan and Tatiana were engaged in a standoff, and Kyle looked pissed.

Declan broke the silence. "This was your idea, Brooks. You deal with her."

With a shake of his head, he left the dining room with Kyle following.

"Deal with her?" she spit out.

"Doll, you really need to chill the hell out. I don't know who fucked you over, I'd assume Monroe. But we're not the enemy. The giant chip on your shoulder is—"

"You keep saying that as if you know me."

"I keep saying it, because it's true. You're making this personal when it's not. No one is trying to fuck with you. You're so ready to be offended you jump to conclusions."

"It may not be personal for you, but it is for me."

"And there's your first problem. The minute you allow a mission to become personal, you're compromised."

Tatiana was shooting daggers at me. Her pretty brown eyes were on fire and she didn't look the least bit interested in what I had to say. But if she had stopped a minute and let go of some of her hostile attitude, she would've seen I wasn't wrong.

"We've shared with you what we know and what we're doing in Bahrain. Why don't you come clean and tell me who you're working for? Maybe we can come up with something that works for all of us."

"Who I work for isn't important."

"I'm trying to help you, Tatiana. What the fuck?"

"I don't need your help, Brooks."

"Um. Doll, you obviously do. You had no idea six of the tablets had been confiscated. And you couldn't find the Bitoo brothers. Without us you're fucked. Mission fail."

Her jaw clenched and through gritted teeth she told me, “I can’t fail.”

“Well, you have. If you want to salvage what you can, explain why keeping Lucre in business is so important.”

“Fuck.”

Her hands scrubbed over her face again and she started to pace. Declan had an op to complete and we were on target to complete our objective. If Tatiana didn’t start talking, tonight after the Bitoo brothers were taken care of, we’d be out of there and off to track down the Saudi prince. Then she’d really be fucked, because whatever intel she could’ve gleaned from his capture would be lost.

As beautiful as I thought she was, as drawn to her as I felt, I wouldn’t compromise my goal for her. Not without good reason.

CHAPTER 9

I had to think. But with Brooks staring at me I couldn't gather my thoughts. I knew I owed him an explanation. I just couldn't think of one that wasn't the truth fast enough. I had to get away from him and come up with a plan, one that didn't involve Brooks muddling with my good sense.

"I need a minute," I told him.

I stood still and fought the urge to fidget under his scrutiny. His piercing gaze was too intense. Not to mention, annoying. I didn't want him studying me. I was too afraid of what he'd figure out.

"If you're thinking about running off, don't."

I bit back a childish retort about him not being the boss of me and instead asked, "Why do you care what I do?"

"Can't answer that, Doll. I just do."

"Can't or won't."

"Can't. You're prickly as fuck. Your attitude in general

sucks. You've done nothing but lie to us. Yet, I still care. I think you're hiding something more than who you work for. I think you've been jacked around and fucked over. So as a way to protect yourself, you come off as a bitch. I believe you like to work alone. Probably because you have trust issues that have made you a control freak. But I do think somewhere in that smart brain of yours you know you need us. But you're too hard-headed to get out of your own way and let us help you. Pride will be your destruction. Mark this, Doll, if you run, I'll find you."

Direct hit. I was right, he saw too much. It was disconcerting. Not even my ex-husband could read me as easily as Brooks had. In the beginning, James had worked for it, he'd put forth the effort to get to know me. But it had taken him years before he fully understood why I did or said certain things and by then he only wanted to know so he could use them as weapons. But not Brooks. He had me pinned in a matter of hours.

He was wrong about one thing, this wasn't about pride so much as it was about revenge. It was personal, and there was no way for me to separate the job from my need for retribution. He may've been right, I was compromised. However, that wasn't going to stop me from finishing what I'd started.

"I'm not going to leave. I just need to think." I picked up my laptop but left the file. It had the information I'd gathered on Falcon and Militrix. "That's for you." I pointed at the documents I'd left and walked out of the dining room.

Before I knew where my feet were taking me, I was in Brooks' room, or mine, as he'd offered it to me if I was going to stay. I sat on the hard mattress and started coming up with a new plan. If the team took out the prince would that really be so bad? Over the last two years I'd been back to work, I'd gathered enough intel to know how his network operated. And wasn't that what my end game was, anyway? When Al Issa was removed as the head figure another person would be put in his place. It wouldn't stop me from tracking the money Lucre dispersed. Why did I care who took out Al Issa? Because I wanted to do it. I wanted the pleasure of being the last person on this earth he saw as he drew his last breath. I deserved it. I was owed at least that much.

Even with the air conditioning blasting in the house I was still sweating. A nice cold shower was exactly what I needed to clear my thoughts of vengeance and figure out my next step. I made my way to the small bathroom attached to the bedroom and stripped down and turned on the tap to cold. Relief washed over me as the lukewarm water cascaded over me. Damn, I missed cold water. Something I'd yet to find in Bahrain. It took a long time but I had a new plan. I was going to have to give Brooks and his team something.

I was actually surprised Tex hadn't figured it out yet, or if he had, why he hadn't passed along the information to the team. The people I worked for were careful, but I supposed the real reason they were able to keep everything secret was because they took credit for nothing. Complete and total deniability. There was no payroll, there was a simple chain of command, and I had no idea who else worked for The Company. We all worked alone, no partners, no teams, we worked our own intel. It was simple really. I was given a mission, told where to apply for a job, magically I was offered whatever job I'd applied for, and I was off. I did work for the UN this time. Before this job I'd worked with different relief organizations, UNICEF, and even the Peace Corps. Temporary jobs that would keep me in whichever region I needed to be in.

I'd never met my handler in person, I only knew him as Leon Brown. Which was a bullshit name, I'd researched him. I was offered a position at The Company after I divorced James and decided to go back to work. My old job at the CIA was a possibility, however when I was presented this opportunity, I took it. I thought working alone was what I needed after everything that had happened with James. A little peace and quiet, no one breathing down my neck telling me I wasn't good enough, wasn't smart enough, wasn't fit enough, my deficiencies were never ending.

Fuck James Monroe. I'd more than been a good wife to him.

I turned off the water and quickly dried off, feeling no less hot than I did before my shower. I grabbed clean clothes out of my bag, put on my shorts and bra, and filled the sink up with water. I'd learned a long time ago to handwash my clothes after wearing them. Perspiration-soaked cotton was not your friend. I was hanging my now rinsed out tee from earlier over the towel rack to dry when I heard it. The swift intake of air and I knew without turning around who was behind me.

Fuck.

"Don't you knock?" I snapped.

"I did. When you didn't answer I thought you bailed again."

"Do you mind? I'd appreciate some privacy."

It was too late. He'd seen them. My heart was thundering in my chest and the room was suffocating.

"Tatiana, darlin'."

"Don't," I bit off. "I don't want your pity."

"The last thing I'm feeling is pity," Brooks told me.

I heard his footsteps come closer. It didn't matter anyway. Close up, far away, you couldn't miss the mess of scars.

"Who did this to you?"

"Doesn't matter."

"The fuck it doesn't. Who?" he growled. "Did Monroe do this?"

"Hell, no." I turned to face him. He'd seen the back, might as well give him the full experience. "Do you think that cocksucker would be breathin' if he did this to me?"

My front was nearly as bad as my back. Brooks' eyes traveled up from my stomach up to my face. I knew what he saw, puckered exit wounds scattered over my torso. When his gaze locked onto mine, I flinched at his angered expression. I'd seen a lot of pissed-off males in my line of work, but never one as furious as him. He looked like a feral beast, and I was a little afraid of him.

"Who. The. Fuck. Did this to you?"

"It was a long time ago."

"I didn't ask you how long ago, Tatiana."

In that moment, him using my name, I missed him calling me Doll. My real name sounded like an expletive the way he snarled it out.

"Al Issa. Not him personally. He's too sophisticated for something as unpleasant as torture, he sent his men to do his dirty work for him."

"Motherfucker!" he roared and stomped out of the bathroom.

So much for my new plan. Time for damage control.

CHAPTER 10

I wanted to commit murder.

No. Scratch that. Murder was too easy. Too fast. I wanted to string up every man that dared to touch Tatiana and torture them they way they'd done her. I'd thought the scars crisscrossing her back had been left from a whip or stick, but when she turned, I'd realized she'd been sliced up and stabbed in the back. Literally. There was so much scar tissue I couldn't tell where one wound had ended and another began.

Inhuman pieces of shit. I'd done a lot in the name of country. Seen a lot more. What I'd never done was brutalized someone. No one on my team had. That's not to say I'd never taken a life, I had, plenty of times. Quick and fast. I had no use for playing with someone. If you were marked for death, it was because you were either trying to actively kill me or my team, or your crimes were so atrocious it warranted the bullet.

But right now, seeing the marks left on Tatiana's beautiful flesh I wanted to hunt and maim. Another piece had clicked into place and I now understood why this was personal for her. Al Issa meant something to her. I just didn't understand why keeping him in power was important. I'd think she'd be happy we'd planned on taking him out.

"What the fuck?" Kyle followed me out of the house into the courtyard.

"Not now," I warned.

"What the hell happened? Did she bail?"

"I said, not now."

"I didn't bail." Tatiana's smooth voice drifted over me. She sounded nothing like the strong woman she had hours before when she was going toe to toe with Dec. She sounded unsure and I didn't like it one bit. "Do you mind if I have a word alone with Brooks?"

"By all means." I heard the door slam behind my friend and I tried to contain my anger.

"It happened two years ago. My second op with The Company. I was in Saudi Arabia just over the Iraqi border," she started. "I had a lead on some items being smuggled out of Iraq, I wanted them before they went to bid. Turned out Lucre wanted them more. I went in to make the buy, so did Al Issa's men. I was taken and held for two days. They left with the items, I was left with the scars."

I couldn't bring myself to speak. I had a hundred questions but I couldn't find my voice. All I could see were the marks on her back. Men had put their filthy hands on her, hurt her. For two days she had to suffer through their brutality.

She sighed and continued, "I thought I was going to die. In and out of consciousness. I actually don't remember a lot of it. Maybe I was passed out, or I'd been able to let go of the pain and go somewhere else. But after they left, I woke up in a home. A man and his wife were tending to my wounds the best they could. I called in for an extraction and was on a plane to Germany within an hour."

Yet, she still wanted to work alone, even after she was captured and tortured. I didn't understand. And who the fuck did she work for that had the capabilities to get to her within an hour of her call for help?

"I was lucky and was able to get medical care before infection set in. I was back in the field in five weeks."

"Five weeks?" She jerked back from my outburst and that pissed me off. "You have no reason to be afraid of me."

"I'm not." Her chin lifted in defiance. I'd give Tatiana Jones one thing, she put on a brave face. She wasn't always truthful, but damn if she didn't fake it.

"Right."

"What's your problem?"

I wasn't sure what my problem was. I'd seen the horrors of war. I, too, bore the marks of battle. I'd seen what humans were capable of doing to each other. I knew. I lived it. I saw it. But seeing it on her was different. Outrageous. Infuriating.

"What's The Company?"

"No way. You don't get to change the subject."

"Someone hurt you."

I stepped closer.

"I'm well aware."

"They cut you."

Another step.

"Again, I know."

"They placed their hands on you with the intention of tormenting you."

Last step and I was face-to-face with her.

"I lived it, Brooks. But nothing happened to me that hasn't happened to hundreds of soldiers, or aid workers, innocent civilians in the wrong place, or hell, to men I'm sure you've worked with. It's a chance we all take. The price we all know we may have to pay if shit goes sideways."

"It shouldn't've happened to you."

"Why not?"

Why not? *Why not?* I didn't have a good answer as to why it should've never happened to her. She was right, we all know the price, and we all go out into the field and take our chances. Yet, the thought of someone harming Tatiana filled me with irrational rage.

I wanted to pull her into my arms and explain my reaction but I couldn't put it into words. It was a gut feeling, something deep in my bones. A sense of protectiveness I'd never felt. An uncharacteristic urge to claim her and shield her from anyone who challenged her safety.

"It just shouldn't've," I lamely told her. "What's The Company?"

She stared at me for a moment, clearly surprised by my lack of verbal communication skills.

"Do you mind if we go in so I only have to explain this once?"

"Sure."

"Are you okay?"

"Not even fucking close," I told her honestly. "Let's go in."

She had nothing to say after that, simply looked at me liked I'd grown a few extra heads and went inside.

Yeah, Doll, I know. I've lost my ever-loving mind.

The guys were already in the dining room. In addition to the maps that had been laid out, the intel she'd left in the folder was, too. She'd done a good job connecting the dots.

"I'm former CIA," she blurted out. "I now work for an off-the-books black ops organization called The Company."

"Never heard of it," Declan said with his brows pulled together.

"No. You wouldn't've. As I said, it's off the books. As in, all of the operatives hold down legitimate employment from various different companies. I am truthfully employed by the UN."

"Who owns it?" That came from Kyle.

"No clue."

"How do you not know who owns The Company? Who hired you?" I asked.

"I was told about it by one of my colleagues at the CIA. He asked me if I was interested in a career move. When I told him I was, he passed my information on, and a week later I was offered a job. No interview. A man named Leon Brown called me, made the offer, explained everything to me, and gave me my first assignment."

"So you're rogue," Declan declared.

"I'm sure the US government would agree with you."

"What's your assignment?"

"Exactly what I told you. Win the auction on the tablets. Once the payment is transferred, we track the money. The Company will see where it's funneled to. Mostly it goes to fund small extremist groups. The up and comers. They are stopped before they can gain traction. Some of the money goes to warlords, the conflicts are good for the smuggling business. Those are typically untouched, those keep the flow of goods."

"But only four tablets remain," I reminded her.

"I've been thinking about that." She started pacing. "I think the Bitoos double-crossed the Lucre and were trying to sell the tablets outside of the auction. I'm not asking for mission specifics, but who sent in the SEALs to recover the artifacts?"

My mind was still spinning on the fact she'd been CIA. And now I was struggling with how much to trust her with, considering she was a good actress. All the bullshit with an off-the-books group, we'd have no way to verify her story. I wondered if Tex knew, or Zane. Tex could find anything on anyone. The Company she supposedly worked for was not in her dossier, neither was her previous employment at the CIA. Those records didn't just vanish. Even if she'd been scrubbed from their database, Tex would've been able to dig and find them. Unless the intel was purposely withheld from us, but why would they do that?

"Special assignment. No other information was given," Declan told her.

"What do you think?" Tatiana turned and asked me.

What did I think? I thought the whole situation was fucked-up. I much preferred a clear and clean cut mission. Black and white. I knew my target and executed my orders. I didn't like this double-cross, who-done-it bullshit. The gray murky area where you had to wade through layers of deceit to get to the truth.

"Given what we know, I'd agree with you," I answered.

Her dark eyes held mine, waiting for me to expand on my curt reply. She'd be waiting a long time. I had nothing to add.

"We found the money trail. So, after tonight we're done?" I asked Declan.

"Not exactly. Mission scope has expanded."

"Expanded?"

"We're waiting on intel validation. Once Tex runs through the new data and confirms it, we're going after Al Issa. Dead or alive. Either way, Zane wants Lucre dismantled." Declan stopped and addressed Tatiana. "I know that's not what you wanted to hear. Someone new will pop up and take over the trade. You'll have a new lead to follow within a week. Omni is too important. Too powerful. Lucre is a cog in the wheel that has to be removed."

Tatiana didn't look pleased. As a matter of fact, she was pissed. Her entire body was vibrating with anger. I wasn't sure how much of it had to do with all of her hard work going in the toilet or if she'd been planning to take out Al Issa and Lucre on her own as payback. Maybe a little of both. I couldn't fault her for wanting revenge. Hell, I wanted to strangle the man with my bare hands for what he'd ordered done to her.

"I need to call this in," she mumbled. "What time are we leaving tonight?"

"Late. The brothers like to drink. We'll wait until after they hit the bar," Declan answered.

"Okay."

Without a glance in my direction she left the room. Four sets of concerned eyes swung my way.

"You good, brother?" Dec was the first to speak.

"Nope."

"What the fuck happened in that room?" Kyle tried to ask again.

I debated how much to tell my team. It wasn't my place to divulge her secrets, but they also needed to understand Tatiana's motivation. Bringing a personal vendetta into an op was dangerous. Not that I was one to talk. In the span of an hour this mission became extremely personal to me as well.

"She was captured and tortured." All four widened their eyes. "Bad. As in, fucked."

"Al Issa?" Thad's voice was thick with anger.

"His men."

The muscle in Max's cheek jumped and his face turned to stone. Not that I'd expected any other reaction from the men on my team. There'd been no doubt they'd be just as pissed as I was. However, their outrage stemmed from very different reasons than mine.

Everything about Tatiana was baffling. I didn't trust a word that came out of her mouth, yet I had no issue going into an uncertain gun fight with her. Saying she was prickly and bitchy was an understatement, yet her attitude was not a turn-off. She was one big IED waiting to explode, yet I wanted to navigate the minefield. She had more emotional and physical scars than any woman I'd come across, yet she was still stunningly beautiful. I wanted to wrap her up and tame her demons. I wanted to touch and kiss every line that marred her flesh. Trace them and learn the story they told. I wanted her so badly my hands twitched and stomach tightened.

I was fucked.

I had to stay away from her. But I knew I wouldn't.

CHAPTER 11

I'd called Leon Brown and briefed him on the current state of play. He agreed and hadn't been surprised the Bitoos tried to double-dip on the tablets. My mission was a bust. If we could recover the four tablets this evening that would be great, but he wasn't holding onto hope. He firmly believed they'd already been sold. I didn't have to tell him the other six had made their way into the hands of the US government. He already knew. I shouldn't have been surprised. Much to my irritation he wanted me to stay with Gold Team. He was making a call to Zane Lewis to clear my attachment to the guys.

Leon felt, if they were going after Lucre, it was best I stay with them. I knew why. The last time I'd gotten too close I almost died. I also knew Leon felt responsible for my injuries. Apparently, he'd visited me at the hospital and he'd stayed a long time. I didn't know that as fact considering I'd been doped up on pain meds and was out of it. Even if my eyes had opened and I saw him sitting there, I didn't remember.

There was a whole lot about the hospital stay and recovery I didn't want to remember, but there were certain pieces I couldn't forget no matter how hard I'd tried. One of those things was the reason why I'd been taken. I'd been cocky. I'd been out to prove myself. I'd spent years getting verbally beat down by my douchebag ex and I wanted to show everyone including myself I was better than what James had thought I was. So, it was my fault, my own insecurities, that led me to be arrogant and I walked right into an ambush. The hit to my pride was almost as bad as the pain. A valuable lesson. One I will never forget.

I glanced up from my laptop when there was a hard knock on the bedroom door.

"Come in."

The door opened and Brooks' large frame came into view. "Sorry. Didn't mean to bang the door down, I wanted to make sure you heard me this time."

Whatever had crawled up his ass seemed to have disengaged, if his smile was any indication. Full lips tipped up, white, straight teeth on display. The only word that came to mind to describe it was dazzling.

"No problem. I was just working. What's up?"

"Wanted to see if you were hungry. Luckily for you Max has KP duty. He grills a mean steak. The only thing Kyle knows how to make is grilled cheese. Declan only makes spaghetti and we've long ago taken Thad off rotation because, well, he can't fuckin' cook to save his life."

"What about you? What's your specialty?"

The dazzling smile turned into something dangerous. Playful. Flirtatious. Panty dropping. I would be in big trouble if he smiled at me like that more often. It was hard staying away from him. Especially after he saw my back and was angry on my behalf. No one in my life knew what I'd gone through. Not my parents, my siblings, or the few friends I had. They couldn't, they all thought I traveled the world working various safe jobs trying to save the world. Sure they knew the places I went weren't all that safe, but they all thought I worked desk jobs. So, no one knew. No one had been there through my recovery. Seeing Brooks so furious made my insides flutter. It was stupid. But it was real. It made it all the more difficult to deny I was attracted to him.

"Daydreaming, again?" He chuckled.

I'd been daydreaming a lot around him. Something I never did. I didn't have the luxury of feeling attraction. Hell, I hadn't felt attractive in a very long time. I was ruined.

And on that thought, I answered, "Yeah, I could eat."

He was eyeing me again, trying to work out what was going on in my head. Good luck with that. Maybe if he could figure it out, he could tell me. I needed to sort myself out and get Brooks out of my head and focus on work.

I closed my laptop and made my way to the door. Brooks hadn't moved. He stayed leaning against the doorjamb. Strong arms folded across his chest, highlighting his muscled pecs and biceps. One cargo pant-covered leg crossed at the ankle. From top to toe he was badboy hot. Chiseled features, strong cheekbones and chin, straight nose, great smile, sexy, unusual eyes. Yeah, he was hot as fuck, and dangerous. Heartbreaker.

"So could I," he murmured.

Full body shiver. That's what his husky voice did to me.

"You should come with a warning label," I told him.

"Yeah? And what should it say?"

Brooks was no longer still, he unfolded his arms, one hand coming to my face, he cupped my cheek, and I leaned into his hold. His thumb stroked my cheek and I'd forgotten what I was going to tell him.

"Danger. Proceed with caution." I finally got the words out.

"I may be dangerous. But I promise, you're in no danger around me." His words came out hushed and thick.

"I don't think that's true, Brooks. I think the reality of you is way better than the fantasy. Making you an imminent threat."

His gaze heated and his lips did this weird twitch. I wasn't sure if he was trying to beat back a smile or a laugh. Either way it made me melt. Apparently, honesty wasn't always the best policy.

"The take away from this conversation was *proceed with caution.*"

"Was?"

"Yeah, babe. Was. Until you told me you'd fantasized about me, about us. Now it's simply, proceed."

"Um. I don't think that's exactly what I meant."

"Yeah, it was. And you're correct. The reality will be far better than anything your mind can conjure up."

"Your arrogance is showing, Brooks."

"No. My confidence is," he returned. "And, Doll, I promise you my kind of certainty means really great things for you."

Brooks' hand was on the move again. His eyes were no longer heated, they were on fire and intense. His hand twisted into my hair, and he slanted my head, right before his lips came down on mine in a mind-blowing kiss. He didn't ask for permission, he plundered. He took what he wanted, how he wanted it. Which was a very good thing, considering he was a good kisser. No, a fucking great kisser. My belly whooshed, my heart pounded in my chest, and my panties dampened. It had been, like never, since I'd been so turned on by a kiss. I wasn't sure if this meant the good things Brooks had promised or if it meant bad things for me. If he could make me come unglued that fast, with one kiss, what would happen if he actually touched me?

I'd spontaneously combust, that's what would happen.

He pulled his mouth from mine but left our bodies touching. His hard-on was hard to miss.

"Jesus," he muttered. "You can fuckin' kiss, Doll."

I wasn't sure if that was a good Jesus, or a bad Jesus. What I did know was, I lacked the brain power to try and figure it out. My mind was preoccupied and I was no longer hungry for food. There was a mattress only a few feet away and I was getting ready to throw caution to the wind and suggest we use it when he spoke again. "You taste so fucking good. I'm a heartbeat away from tossing your fine ass on that bed, but the guys are waiting for us to eat."

Thank god.

Thank god, my mind was muddled and I wasn't thinking clearly.

I tried to pull back but Brooks' hand on my hip tightened. "I want you to know we're leaving this room under extreme protest." My eyes locked on his and they were no less intense than they were before he kissed me. "We will be finishing this." I swallowed the lump in my throat and nodded. Because, what else could I do? I wanted to finish it. "No way I get a taste of you and not go back in for seconds. And by seconds, Doll, I mean, with my mouth between your legs, *tasting* you."

Did he just say that? He did. He said he was going to put his mouth between my legs. Was it possible for someone to orgasm by verbal stimulation? Because my sex was clenching and I needed a change of panties.

"I see you like that idea. And as much as I want to explore that now, I need to feed you and we need to prep for tonight's mission."

Shit. Right. Work. We had work to do.

"Damn, you're pretty."

I don't think anyone had called me pretty since I was a child. It was nice. Brooks' sweet side was far more dangerous than the sexy badboy with a dazzling smile.

I was fucked.

CHAPTER 12

I couldn't take my eyes off Tatiana.

Hands down the most beautiful woman I'd laid eyes on. But when she came out of my room after dinner with a pair of black cargos on, black boots, and a tight-fitting tee, I nearly swallowed my tongue. When she strapped on a SERPA thigh rig and holstered her Sig, my dick jerked in my pants. And when she strapped on a bullet-proof tac vest, precome leaked from my dick and I was sure there was a wet spot. Her hair was pulled up in a high ponytail, leaving her sexy neck exposed for my viewing pleasure. And it was a pleasure. I couldn't wait to suck and nibble on the soft skin around her throat and neck. Dec gave her an ear piece, and after a comm check, we'd be ready to roll.

Now we were less than a quarter mile to the warehouse where the Bitoos were holed up and Declan, Thad, Kyle, and Max had broken away to get into their positions, leaving Tatiana and me to walk the last bit by ourselves.

The area wasn't particularly shit nor was it a nicer part of Bahrain. The building was waterfront, though there were no boat docks. As we approached the industrial park, I was happy to see it was deserted.

"Set and ready," Kyle informed the team.

"Sixty feet and closing in," Declan returned. "Team two, you in position?"

"Affirmative. Waiting for the green light," I answered.

"You good?" I asked Tatiana.

"Yep."

She had her weapon up and was scanning the area. There should've been nothing sexy about her appearance. Her curves were hidden behind tactical gear, a balaclava covered her beautiful face, and a bulletproof brain bucket hid her shiny long hair. Nothing outwardly appealing, yet she was turning me on like no other woman ever had.

"Breach." Declan came through my comms once again.

I waited for the heavy breathing of a firefight and the telltale sounds of rapid gunfire. Nothing. Silence as they made their way clearing the building. The only communication was them calling in "clear" as they went. Something wasn't right.

"Sniper, you got anything?" I asked Kyle.

"Negative."

"We got blood," Max announced.

"Team two, you're clear to move in."

Tatiana nodded from beside me, allowing me to take the lead, and we covered the last of the distance to the building. I could feel her at my back matching me step for step as we moved at a fast clip. We entered the door the team used, bringing us into a small but empty room. Off to the right there were three doors, all open. Max and Declan were standing in the doorway of one of the rooms and Thad was at the back door. Blood was everywhere.

We were too late.

"Fuck," Tatiana mumbled. "Totally fucked."

"Looks like one was taken out there." Declan pointed to a pool of blood on the cement floor, the splatter on the wall suggesting he was correct. "One in the first room."

"The others?"

That only accounted for the possibility that two out of the five brothers had been shot. With no bodies there was no way to confirm.

"Fuck, man, you got me. This room is a mess." He gestured to the room he was standing in front of.

I broke away from Tatiana and peeked inside. He wasn't lying. It looked like a massacre had taken place. The stench of coppery blood was thick in the air.

"There's only four drag smears," Tatiana noted.

We turned to look and she was correct. Four very distinct blood trails led to the back door.

"Sniper, how's the back look?" Declan asked.

"You're clear."

Thad opened the back door, trying but failing not to step in the blood as he stepped out. Max, Declan, and Tatiana followed and I pulled up the rear. The blood trail continued the short distance to the water's edge. The drop down wasn't very far, maybe three feet into the shallow water.

"Got one," Dec called in.

Timothee Bitoo was floating below, face up.

It took less than ten minutes to find the other four Bitoos all suffering their brother's fate. It would've been considered a good night, someone else coming in and doing the dirty work of disposing of the brothers, but Tatiana didn't get the interrogation she needed and the tablets were not in the building. Neither was anything else helpful. So all in all it was a bust. We got nothing.

The drive back to the compound was silent. Tatiana sat next to me and I could feel her annoyance rolling off of her in waves.

We were pulling into the compound when she finally spoke. "Have you talked to Zane about me going to Saudi Arabia with you?"

"He mentioned it. But the details haven't been worked out yet," Dec answered.

He had spoken to the team about the possibility of Tatiana staying with us for a while. The team had a meeting and discussed her continued presence. Zane wouldn't entertain the idea unless the team agreed and felt like she'd add value to the mission. Everyone gave their okay and volleyed the decision back to our boss.

"What details?"

Tatiana was going to be pissed. It might've made me a pussy but I was pleased I wasn't the one having to explain what the details were.

"We'll discuss them when we get inside."

Nothing further was said as we exited the car and each of us removed our boots before we entered the house. We may've been a team of mercenaries, but no one, not even us, wanted brain matter and blood tracked into the house.

Tatiana made a beeline to the bedroom. She was already in a bad mood and irritated. No doubt she was going be a whole lot more of both of those things, but I followed. All my shit was still in the room and I needed a shower and a change of clothes.

She had her tac vest off and tossed on the bed when I entered the room. Her eyebrow lifted in question as she unbuckled her thigh holster.

"Sorry, Doll, only shower downstairs."

I made my way through the bedroom, into the bathroom and started to undress. The area was so small I had to unload my gear and dump it in the sink. Christ, I missed man-sized American bathrooms. I was down to my boxer briefs when Tatiana filled the doorway.

"Do you know what the details are?" she asked.

So maybe she wouldn't be pissed I was invading what I told her was going to be her room.

"Zane didn't discuss the particulars but I can guess."

"And what's your guess?"

"Can we do this after I shower?"

"What, you can't multitask?"

Oh, I could multitask. I took her in and noted the challenging glint in her eye. Game on. I dropped my underwear, gave her my back, and turned the taps on, before I turned back to talk to her.

"My guess would be Zane wants more background intel on you."

"Why?"

I had to hand it to her. Her eyes hadn't dropped below my chest. She was fighting it though. I had no issue standing in front of her nude. She could take in her fill and I'd be perfectly comfortable with her doing so.

"Why?" I returned, stepping in the shower, not bothering to close the clear plastic curtain.

"Yes. Why? I've told you everything you need to know."

"You didn't scratch the surface, Doll. The team vote was to bring you along. Zane will take that into consideration but only after he gets a full work-up on you and The Company. No chance in hell is he sending you in with us without knowing who you work for."

I lathered the soap in my hands and went to work washing the sweat and stench away when she appeared within touching distance. And she looked just as mad as I knew she'd be.

"Leon Brown will never give him the information he's after," she informed me. "I should cut out now so I can figure out my next move."

My soapy hand grabbed her bicep before she could leave. Her eyes dropped to where I was holding her and I waited for her to demand I let go. Her gaze snapped to mine but instead of seeing irritation, I saw heavy lids and heat shining back.

"You'd be surprised what Zane Lewis can find out."

The way she was looking at me, I didn't think she comprehended what I'd said. She was back to daydreaming. Fantasizing. And on that thought, my dick swelled. I gave her arm a tug and to my surprise she stepped forward, fully clothed into the shower.

Her body collided with mine and I wasted no time. My mouth was on hers and she immediately opened. This kiss was no less forceful than the first, but it had a hint of familiarity to it. Her tongue brushed mine and it was like it was welcoming me home. This time I didn't stop myself from touching her. My hands were everywhere. I ripped her shirt off, forcing her hands up as the fabric cleared her head. I tossed the cotton aside and moments later her bra followed. My head bent and I latched onto a pink nipple. One hand on her ass, the other curled around her ponytail pulling her head back, making her arch her chest.

"You've got great tits, Doll," I muttered before moving to the other side.

Her hands were steadily working, trying to get her pants off. Once they were around her ankles and she was kicking them loose, her hands moved to my ass and she squeezed. I moaned against her skin before I lifted my head and slammed my lips back onto hers.

I wanted to taste and touch every part of her. I couldn't get enough. I'd never wanted to fuck a woman so badly, yet I also wanted to take my time and savor everything about her. Fast. Slow. Now. Later. I couldn't make up my mind. I wanted it all. Now and later. Fast then slow.

One of her hands moved between us. There was nothing gentle in the way she fisted my dick. Small fingers wrapped around my shaft and violently jerked. It should've been painful but it was raw and needful. I shoved her panties to the side and found treasure. Hot, slick, wet treasure. I slipped a finger inside, pulled out, and slid back in two. She stroked my dick and I fingered her pussy until we were both moaning our pleasure.

I pulled my hand away, hitched her leg high, and

waited. She guided the tip of my dick to her opening and I slammed home.

"Christ," I moaned.

"Brooks." Her moan was breathy but no less demanding.

The sweet sound of sex filled the bathroom, coupled with the sound of water splashing between us. Hard. Fast. Heaven. So damn good, the lukewarm water doing nothing to cool my heated skin. My body was on fire, my entire being solely focused on the feel of her as she took me.

"Please don't stop," she begged.

"I can feel you, Tatiana. You're there. Come on, baby. Come with me."

I pounded into her the best I could in the small space I was provided. Later, I'd take my time, enjoy making her squirm and scream. For now, it was a race to completion. Her pussy was contracting, threatening to unman me.

"Brooks! Oh, shit. Oh, God. There."

"Mouth," I growled and she leaned forward to kiss me.

I swallowed her groans as she fell over the edge. Three strokes later I planted deep and joined her.

I didn't break the kiss for a long time, letting us both come down from our shared ecstasy. When she finally pulled back, her features were gentled and her eyes soft and I knew I'd been right. There wasn't much a man wouldn't give to have that look. I was so fucked.

CHAPTER 13

I tried to school my features. Hide from Brooks' penetrating stare, but I couldn't. The mask I'd perfected over the years refused to fall into place. And when he smiled, I knew I was in trouble. My leg was still around his hip, his strong hand holding my thigh where he wanted it. His other hand on the side of my neck, thumb grazing over my throat.

I was such a slut. God. Ohmygod. I couldn't even blame him for some crazy seduction. All it had taken was a tug of my arm and I'd stepped into the shower with him and threw myself at the man. What was wrong with me? Now I was looking at him like some love-sick teenager. Damn. What now? Do I say thank you? That was great, see ya around? He must have thought I was a slut, because, well, I was one.

"What has you thinking so hard, Doll?"

"How do you do that?"

A sexy smirk played on his lips. Totally arrogant.

"Do what?"

"Know when I've drifted off."

"Oh, that." He smiled. "Your eyes. They lose focus."

"Um. I didn't know that."

He slowly let my leg down and I tried not to whimper when his dick slipped free. He chuckled and leaned forward, kissing my neck where his hand had just been. Before he pulled back, his tongue touched the skin there. Nice. Another kiss below my ear, my cheek, then my lips. It wasn't as long and wet like the others. It was gentle and sweet. A touch of his mouth but it was no less powerful. I was so screwed.

"Grab the soap and I'll wash you."

His request pulled me back from whatever dream world I'd been living in. Hell no, he wasn't washing me. Not only, hell no, fuck no. Sex up against a wall was one thing. He couldn't touch my scars while my back was pressed to the tile behind me. And with us so close, he probably couldn't see the ones on my abdomen clearly.

What the fuck had I done? Now that the fog had disappeared I realized that once he stepped away, I'd be on full display. How was I supposed to get out of the shower unseen?

"Whoa. Tatiana. What's wrong?"

"Nothing."

"Don't bullshit me."

"Nothing."

Wrong answer. The lips that had gently kissed me moments ago were two hard flat lines. His jaw flexed. His brows pulled together.

"Do. Not. Bullshit. Me. Not even five minutes ago I

had my dick inside of you and you panting your orgasm in my mouth. Then I got the sweetest look I'd ever seen. You don't get to put that hand back up and bullshit me."

"You're unbelievable. You think because you had your *dick inside of me*, you get to boss me around? And demand I tell you my every thought?"

"No, Doll, I get to demand that because when we were done your face said it all. Told me everything your mouth won't. So I'm asking you again. What's wrong? Did I hurt you?"

The last part of his question deserved an answer. "You didn't hurt me."

"So tell me why your face went from soft and relaxed to high alert?"

"No reason. Brooks. Damn. There's nothing wrong. I don't need you to wash me, I just want to get out."

Wrong thing to say, again. His gaze became knowing and I involuntarily stiffened. So much for acting unaffected. He knew exactly what I'd been thinking.

"I don't care about your scars."

Punch to the stomach.

"Well, I do," I snapped.

"Baby, you are absolutely gorgeous."

"Save the bullshit, Brooks. You already got in my pants. No need to sweet talk me."

"Honest to God, woman. Honest to God. I thought you had a chip on your shoulder. I was wrong. You have a fucking boulder sitting there. Do you really think I need to sweet talk you? Do I look like I need to blow smoke up a woman's ass to get laid?"

Jerk. Arrogant prick.

"Right. Badboy, hot guy, Brooks doesn't have a problem getting laid. I bet there's no shortage of women who would love a roll with you."

His eyes narrowed into tiny slits. "You'd be correct. There is no shortage. However, women throwing themselves at me to say they'd been laid by a SEAL long ago lost its appeal. I do not go around saying flowery shit, in hopes to get my dick wet. I'm going to tell you this one more time. You are hot as fuck. When you forget to be a bitch, you're beautiful. And right after you come, when your face is lazy, and your eyes are gentle, you are by far the most stunning woman I've ever seen. So you can spew your venom and try and pollute what we just shared, but it will not change the fact that the scars on your back take nothing away from you. As far as I see it, they tell me more about the woman you are. And, Doll, I like what they say."

Once he was done verbally beating me into a bloody pulp, he left the shower, grabbed a towel, and was out of the bathroom. Shit. It took me two point five seconds to feel like a complete bitch, and seconds more to mourn the loss of his presence. I hadn't even had the chance to appreciate all of his finely-sculpted muscles and the fact that he'd made me feel more desirable in the short time we were together than any man, ever.

I owed him an explanation.

I finished my shower and quickly dried off and went into the bedroom. He was gone. Of course he was, I'd been a royal asshole to him—again. I found the clothes I'd had on before we went out on the unsuccessful op and went in search of the guys. Okay, I went looking for

Brooks, but if he was already out talking with the team, I'd missed my chance to apologize to him.

I found them in the living area lounging on the two well-worn large sofas. All eyes came to me and suddenly I was very aware there was a possibility they'd heard us having sex in the shower. Declan was on the phone and he was the first to look away, but the other four stared.

Oh, shit.

"Come here, Doll." Brooks broke the silence.

I shook my head not wanting to get too close. "What's going on?"

"Word is Al Issa retrieved the tablets from the Bitoos. The auction has been cancelled."

"Shit. What now?"

"Abort. Regroup. Reengage."

"And where does that leave me?"

I hated that I sounded so uncertain. If Zane wasn't going to approve me joining the team, I needed to get to work. Finding someone to take me into Saudi Arabia wouldn't be difficult but it would cost a mint. I'd need a day or two to get the money sorted. I'd also need to hurry and start setting up a support network. I still had contacts I'd used before but they'd need to be mobilized. And that took time.

Before Brooks could answer, Declan stood and held the phone in my direction. "Here."

I took the phone and placed it to my ear. "Hello."

"Tatiana Jones. Long time."

"If it isn't the pain in my ass, Zane Lewis," I returned.

His chuckle reminded me that he, too, thought I was a pain in the ass. The last time I saw him was on a Russian op when I was still in the CIA. The mission was fucked. He and one of his operatives, Laura Bennett, now known as Jasmin Parker, were captured and almost killed. I liked Laura. I was the one who had scrubbed her records and had given her a new identity. I'd also worked with her husband, Lincoln Parker, on a human trafficking case. He, too, was a good operative.

"I heard you retired when you got hitched to that douchebag Monroe."

God, I hated to be reminded of my monumental lapse in judgement.

"You heard correct."

"Glad you got shot of his ass."

That may've been the nicest thing Zane had ever said to me. The man shared and showed no emotion.

"Yeah, me, too. So, you have concerns with me joining your team on this op?"

"I did. I spoke to Leon Brown. We cleared some shit up. He offered your help. Tex confirmed the information he gave us. But before I clear you, I have some questions."

"Wait. Leon gave you information? What he'd tell you?"

"Not at liberty to discuss that with you."

What the fuck?

"Come again?"

"Don't bitch at me, woman. You're the one that took the job. If you have the need to know more, ask."

Did he think I hadn't tried that?

"What are your questions?"

"You gonna be able to keep your shit wired tight, you get close to Al Issa?"

"If you mean, will I be able to not put a bullet between his eyes, then no. You asking if I can be professional and have the team's back, then yes."

"Heard about that, too. Have to say, what you went through—"

"I was there," I growled.

"Good to see you're the same bitch you've always been."

In Zane Lewis's world, 'bitch' was high praise.

"What else do you need?"

"You straight with Brooks?"

My eyes shot to Brooks before they slid to Declan. Yeah, they'd heard. And Declan had reported in. Such a damn slut.

"I'm straight," I bit out.

Zane didn't chuckle. He outright roared with laughter. "Right."

"I heard some things, too, Z. Heard you're now having heart-to-hearts and found yourself a woman."

His laughter died and he answered, "Found myself the perfect woman. And the day I start having heart-to-hearts is the day I hand in my balls."

"So that last question? The purpose?"

"Just doing a head check."

"My head is fine."

"Right. And if that changes, you let me know."

"Copy that, *boss*."

"Now you're in the spirit. This mission goes well, we might be able to work something out."

"I have a job," I reminded him.

"You do. But let's just say, I'm a better option."

"What do you know?" I tried again.

"More than you, less than I should."

"That's not a damn answer."

"It's the only one you're gonna get."

"Glad to see you're the same ass you've always been."

Zane was a lot of things, an asshole being one of them. What he wasn't was a liar. He was a straight shooter, to the point of being rude. He didn't say anything to spare feelings. He pulled no punches. If he was telling me working for him was a better option than working for The Company, then he found something he didn't like about the group. That worried me.

"We'll be in touch. In the meantime, you're one of us. You take your team's back. Declan is the team leader. His word is law."

"Christ, Z, you make it sound like I haven't been in this business damn near as long as you."

"No. You've been in the spy business. Where there is no loyalty. You people will disavow motherfuckers faster than I can blink. You're a damn good operator, but your ability to be a part of a team is yet to be seen. Any of those men in that room will take a bullet for you. You let that settle in and think on it. If you can't return the favor, get your shit, and good luck to you."

"I got it."

"Good. Don't let my men get dead."

Nothing but dead air. In true Zane fashion, he had the last word.

I handed Declan back his phone and fought the urge to punch the rat bastard in his stomach.

"Damn, it's like she's been a part of the team for years." Max laughed.

"If I had a dollar for every time I heard someone call Z an asshole, I'd be retired living the good life. How long have you known Zane?" Kyle asked.

"A long time. I knew of him long before I met him in person. Russia was the last op I worked with him. After what happened, he refused to execute anymore CIA contracts. Not that I blamed him. That mission was a whole lotta fucked-up. Too much intel was held back. Bad plays were made. Jasmin and Zane caught the shit end of it. I worked with Linc after that. Almost two years behind the scenes on his trafficking case. I've worked with Leo and Eric, too."

"Why'd you leave the CIA?"

My lungs seized and my brain told me to tell Thad to mind his own business. But I couldn't, not when I couldn't forget what Zane had said – these men would take a bullet for me. Not because they knew me, simply because I was a part of their team for this mission.

"Monroe asked me to."

"The fuck?" Brooks grumbled.

"He said he wanted a family but my work was too dangerous. When he asked, things were still good between us. I wanted kids, so I agreed. After I quit, he found having a wife at home was too much for him. Things got bad. Let's just say he's a *keep my private life and personal life separate* kinda man." Brooks stared at me, clearly not understanding my reference. I went on, "It's rather difficult to hide your other women when your ex-CIA wife is home full-time."

"He cheated on you." Declan observed.

"Too many to count."

"Too many to count," Brooks repeated.

"In San Diego there's a Frog Hog on every corner waiting to suck a Team Guy's dick. He wasn't even careful about it. He'd come home smelling like various different perfumes telling me he was working late. He'd already been sidelined from being deployed, so he was babysitting tadpoles at X-Division. He hated that command. The longer he was there the more of an asshole he became."

"Fucking disgrace," Max said. "Why didn't you call his command? He would've been court marshaled and chaptered out."

"Not the kinda woman who fucks with a man's career. He did me dirty, but still, I'm a big girl. I didn't need to go tattle to his commander."

"You would've done the teams a favor. No one wants a cheat at their back. A man can fuck over the woman he's promised to love, he has no problem stabbing you in the back," Thad told me.

He was right about James. He had no problem breaking our vows, but he did have his team's back. He was all about his team. He lived for the next mission. He believed he was the best man on the team and they wouldn't survive unless he was there. He was a narcissist prick. Better than everyone else.

I was done sharing, so I asked, "Any of you been married?"

I got four nos and a mumbled response from Declan. I was getting ready to ask him to repeat his answer but when I looked at him, I stopped myself. Pain clear as day. I wasn't sure if it was because he'd wanted to but never had married or if he had and was divorced. Whichever it was, I wasn't touching it.

I felt like I had to come clean with the team on one more topic. "I have full workups on all of you. Nothing personal. I only went through your service records. I don't know how much Tex gave you on me, but if you have any questions, I'll answer."

"Remember that first day we met you and you and Brooks were sparring?" Thad chuckled. "You said your accomplishments weren't important. Care to share now?"

"Same as most of you. Only without all the dive, that's water and air both, master quals. Master range officer, rifle and pistol. I went through modified sniper training. Close quarter combat, hand-to-hand. Same training you got at BUD/s." I added the last part just to ruffle their feathers.

It didn't take long for the banter to start. All of them calling bullshit on my statement.

"I don't know, boys. Every facet of SEAL school has been publicized and made into History Channel documentaries. It's pretty tough but no one really knows what happens at The Farm. For all you know, it's harder."

I couldn't hold back my laugh when the four former SEALs' mouths opened and shut not knowing what to say.

"That's the dumbest thing I've ever heard." Kyle was the first to break. "A fuckin' documentary doesn't tell you shit."

"Like to see you try and get through Hell Week," Thad added.

"Only those of us with the testicular fortitude to endure extreme conditions made it through," Brooks said and I burst out laughing again.

I had been waiting for Declan to put in his two-cents. He was Army, not Navy. Former Force Recon, who had been recruited to the CIA and had trained at The Farm. But he remained silent. Which was puzzling. I wondered if his team knew he'd been with the agency. They all seemed tight, and it didn't seem like something he'd keep from them. But if he was, then he had his own reasons for doing so and I'd keep my mouth shut.

"All right, all right. Sheesh. BUD/s is tougher than The Farm," I gave in.

"You really don't know anything about who you work for?" Thad inquired.

I wouldn't say his tone was accusatory but more inquisitive.

"No. And from what Zane just told me, I'm beginning to question the sagacity of my decision. I took the job because I wanted to work alone. I needed time to put my life after James back together."

"What happened when you were captured?" That was from Declan.

The whimper that followed was unintentional. I cut my eyes to Brooks, ready to lambast him for sharing something that was not his business to share. But I found he wasn't looking at me, he was staring at Declan. And he was pissed.

"How much do you know?" I asked.

"Just what Zane told me. You were following a lead on some artifacts coming out of Iraq into Saudi Arabia. You were ambushed by some men who were with Lucre and they had you for two days."

"Then you know everything," I told him.

"Right."

"What do you want, Declan? You wanna see what they left me with? It's not pretty. Forty-eight hours they played with me. Two fucking days they whipped me, knifed me, tied me up, laughed at me. And when they were done, they walked out with four relics all under three inches. All four pieces could fit in your hand. That's what they wanted. Toying with me? That was nothing but fun for them. So again, you know everything. There's nothing more to the story. They found me, took me, scarred me, and nearly took my life."

Four angry growls came from the men. I couldn't handle anymore. Q and A was over.

"Tatiana—"

"Don't, Declan. I get it. You're protecting your team. I don't have any motivation other that the mission at hand. My assignment was to win an auction, then move on to some ancient cones coming up for sale. My orders have shifted and I'm on board."

"I just wanted to know if we get to a place where we're hauling Al Issa's ass in, if you'll be okay."

"Then I'll tell you the same thing I told Zane. I see Al Issa, I'm puttin' a bullet in his head. He owes me more than a pound of flesh for what his men did to me. I live every day in a body that is desecrated because of him. I'm taking my payment."

"They violate you?" Brooks' low growl had me rocking back on my heels.

"Violate?"

"Rape you?" he clarified.

"No. They were having too much fun carving me up. Making sure every time I saw what they left me, I'd be disgusted."

"Nothing disgusting about you, Doll."

"Right. Everyone loves to see skin that looks like a cheese grater's been taken to it."

"Those marks are a reminder of how strong you are. What you went through and came out even stronger."

"I'd rather not have the reminder."

"And I'd rather you didn't as well. But you do, and they're fucking beautiful."

He was too close. I needed him to step back before I did something stupid like wrap my arms around his waist and bury my face in his chest. "Every line on your back a testament to your strength. Every scar a reminder you *are* breathing. You get that shot, take it. But, baby, it's not going to make the scars disappear. Only you can do that. And you do it by embracing them. Not one fuckin' thing disgusting about you."

I wanted to argue with him, remind him of what he'd seen when he saw me with my shirt off. How gross my back looked, but I couldn't. I was too fucking tired. Bone-deep tired. Emotionally drained from talking about the two worst topics in my life. Why didn't they want to know the easy stuff like my family life, where I'd grown up, if I had siblings? Questions that wouldn't put me on the brink of a nervous breakdown.

I just wanted to crawl into bed and sleep. The scariest part was, I wanted Brooks curled behind me holding me tight. Maybe it wasn't a good idea tagging along with the team. Maybe I needed a clean break.

CHAPTER 14

Tatiana had murmured her goodnights and went back into the bedroom. No one spoke until the door closed behind her.

"What the fuck?" I turned to Dec.

"Everyone in this room had the right to know where her head was at about what happened to her."

"I agree. Think maybe a word with her in private first would've been the cool thing to do?"

Declan's features went hard and I knew he was gearin' up to say something that was going to piss me the hell off. "Let me ask you this. If I questioned a man the same way I questioned her, would your balls be twisted? Or a better question, if you weren't fuckin' her and I inquired about an operation that went south. One that has the same players as the one we're getting ready to walk her into, would you be pissed?"

"Fuck It's not—"

"Yes, Brooks, it's exactly like that. I'm not going to

pretend to understand." Declan's hands went up. "I know nothing about love, feelings, emotional shit. I watched the big, bad Zane Lewis fall in love, I suppose it's possible for a jackass like you to do it, too. But do not let that shit get in the way of my mission again. I wasn't trying to hurt or embarrass her. I knew the mission specifics but I needed to know if we walked her into Lucre if she'd be on a suicide mission to get to Al Issa. That happens, we're all fucked. I need to know she has the capability to keep her shit in check and take someone's back. If one or all of us has to babysit her, she's of no use."

I wasn't paying attention after he said love. Who the hell said anything about falling in love? She was hot. A phenomenal kisser and was great in bed. Or in the shower as it were. Bottom line was, I was thinking with my dick, not my heart. No one said anything about feelings. I was pretty sure she'd said she didn't want complicated, either. Emotions were a complication. No. We were two adults that had engaged in a mutually beneficial activity and I planned on engaging in it plenty more.

"You said it was fucked, but you didn't say how fucked," Thad said in a hushed voice.

"About as bad as she described it, minus the disgusting part. There's probably not a square inch of her back that isn't scarred. Through and through to her stomach. Honestly, I don't see how she lived. Half of the wounds should've killed her."

"Fucking hell," he growled.

"Damn," Kyle mumbled.

"It's been two years and I can tell you she was left with more than just the physical scars. That shit marked her deep. Monroe did, too. She acts bitchy as a way to protect herself, one hand up warding off anyone from getting too close."

"You gonna help her with that?" Max asked.

"With what?"

"With dropping that hand?" I didn't answer and he sighed. "You said it yourself, the asshat Monroe left her with the need to protect herself. She doesn't need you dickin' her around."

"You think I'd dick her around?"

"You weren't exactly quiet in the shower. You haven't hidden the fact there's.... something...whatever that is, between the two of you. So, yes, brother, I think you'd dick her around. Unintentionally."

"I'm handling it."

"Hope so. That woman has been through enough."

Now he was pissing me way the hell off. I'd never given anyone on my team reason to think I'd fuck over a woman. My days of picking up women in a bar for a quickie in my truck were long over. Therefore, I told him, "You're pissing me the fuck off." I did this on a growl. I also did this in a way there was no mistaking he'd, Pissed Me The Fuck Off.

"I can see that," Max returned, completely unfazed by my annoyance.

"I'll tell you one last time, I'm handling it—with care."

On a nod he announced, "I'm hitting the head, then hittin' the sack. I'm wiped."

The rest of the team, except Declan, murmured their goodnights and headed off to their rooms.

"You straight?" he asked when we were alone.

"I am. Are you?" His head tilted and he stared at me. "Your first op as team leader. It isn't exactly going as planned," I reminded him.

"Nothing ever goes as planned."

This was true. Even the best planned ops always had some sort of hiccup. One of the many reasons we had backup plans for our backup plans.

"And Tatiana? You okay with her taggin' along?"

"I knew her before she quit the CIA. Well, not personally, more I knew of her. My area of focus was Central and South America, hers was the Middle East. That doesn't mean I didn't hear a lot about her. She had a stellar reputation. Smart, quick on her feet. Great with human assets and information gathering. She and Monroe met on a mission."

"No shit?"

"Rumor has it, she flat out laughed in his face and turned him down. He worked at it. Took him months after they got back stateside to get her to agree to go out for drinks. Then months after that to nail her down and get her to commit. And when I say worked at it, he pulled out all the stops. He may be an asshat, lying scumbag, but he knew how to turn on the charm and wear her down. Around the CIA she was known as the Ice Queen. No one got close. So this, what's going on between the two of you, the fact she's let you in, both literally and figuratively. No matter how small." He smirked and went on. "Is not her normal MO. So when you say you're handling her with care, I hope you mean with kid gloves."

I thought about what he said. He was wrong, not that I would correct him. Tatiana didn't need kid gloves, she'd see right through that play and it'd piss her off. She needed honesty.

"I have it under control."

Dec sighed and shook his head. "I hope so. That woman has a short temper and the potential to decimate you."

"Me?"

"You're not real good at hiding your shit, brother. When Zane told me what happened to her, your earlier shit hemorrhage made sense. You saw her scars."

I was going to deny that I'd had a shit hemorrhage but I couldn't. His description was better than me telling him I wanted to commit murder.

"I'd have that reaction with anyone."

"Bull-fucking-shit. You've seen my scars. You didn't look like you were ready to punch a wall. You've seen Zane's. You've seen the bullet holes in Max's chest. None of those times upon seeing the marks or hearing the story did you look like you were on the war path."

Shit. Goddamn, he was right. Time to move on.

"I got my shit sorted. I'm callin' it a night."

"Sleep well." He chuckled.

I flipped him the middle finger over my shoulder, not bothering to look back as I made my way to the bedroom. The room I was now sharing with Tatiana. I may've told her I'd take the couch, but shit had changed. Time to adapt and shift.

I gently closed the door behind me, not wanting to wake her. My efforts were for naught. Tatiana sat up in bed and even though it was dark in the room, I could feel her eyes on me.

"What are you doing?"

"Hittin' the sack. I'm fuckin' beat."

"In here? I thought you were taking the couch."

Knowing she couldn't see me, I smiled and dropped my pants, kicking them to the side. I yanked off my tee and tossed that, too. I knew she'd be pissed I was joining her and I was looking forward to her sassy mouth telling me all the reasons I needed to get out of her bed.

I crawled in, leaving her no option to move over.

"Brooks," she hissed.

"There's more than enough room in here."

"That's not the point."

"Then what is?"

I tucked a pillow under my head, turned to the side, tagged her around her waist, and pulled her back to my front. When she struggled, I tightened my hold and curved my body around hers.

"You can't sleep in here."

"Why not?"

"It's totally inappropriate."

"And me fucking you in the shower wasn't?"

"Brooks," she hissed again, making me smile some more.

I kissed the top of her head and told her, "You don't strike me as the type of woman who gives a shit what anyone else thinks. I sure as fuck don't. So why start now?"

"I'm not a slut."

I tried to stop my body from tightening, I failed. Every muscle bunched. I hated that word and it pissed me off she was inferring I thought she was one.

"I know you're not."

"Right. I gave it up easy. And the guys heard. If that doesn't scream slut, I don't know what does."

I pulled back, rolled her to her back, and even though I knew she couldn't see me, I got face-to-face with her.

"No one. I repeat, no one in this house thinks you're a slut."

I could feel her breath on my lips and I wanted to close the distance and taste her, but this was important. I needed to know she understood.

CHAPTER 15

He was too close. His lips lingered a scant distance above mine and I wanted him to kiss me. Which was a bad idea. Because kissing would turn into something else, and that would to lead to even more something, then I'd be a double slut. And the guys would probably hear again.

I knew this. I knew it was a bad idea. So what the hell was wrong with me? Why did I want him to lean down, just a tiny bit more, and take my mouth? Because I was a double slut, that's why.

Instead of closing the distance I mumbled, "Right."

"I will never understand society, women especially. A man goes after what he wants and gets himself some, no one thinks twice about it. A woman takes what she wants, and other women call her a slut. Which leads her to call herself a slut. Which only further makes her think poorly of herself for doing something that is not wrong. And if she's lucky, she had a good time doing it. So I will tell you again. No one in this house thinks you're a slut. And most especially not me. I don't care if you took one look at me, thought to yourself, *I'm going to fuck him,* and two minutes later you went about doing it. That makes you a woman who knows what she wants. A woman who will take it and not give a shit what anyone else thinks about what she's doin'. Nowhere in that does it mean you are a slut."

Well, I now knew his view of women's sexuality and how they treat one another. It still didn't change the fact I had taken one look at him and the fantasies began—in earnest.

"All right, Brooks. Then I'll rephrase. I'm easy."

"Wrong again. There is nothing easy about you."

"Yeah. Okay. The first time I let you kiss me you were just coming in the room to tell me dinner was ready. The next time, I walked straight into the shower fully clothed and without thought about anything, including safe sex, I let you fuck me against a wall. All of that not only screams 'easy' it screams sl—"

"Tatiana," he warned.

I ignored him and continued, "It took James months before I let him kiss me. And after that it was another month before I let him touch me."

"That says more about him than you."

"How the hell do you figure that?"

"Doll." He said "doll" in a way that was more like him calling me dumb than saying my name.

"That's not an answer."

"It says you knew you needed to go slow and protect yourself from him. You were cautious, slow, calculating. It also says he's an idiot. In more ways than one. When a man finds a woman like you, he does not delay making you his. It does not take months to get in there. And when he finally ties you to him, he does not act like a dick and step out on you. He recognizes what he has, and fights like hell to keep it."

"I can't argue with you about him being an idiot. But it wasn't just him. I've always been cautious and slow."

"Then you never found the right kind of man."

"Uh huh, and let me guess, you're the right kinda man?"

"When you first saw me, what was your first thought?"

Oh, no. We weren't going there. There were some things a girl didn't divulge. First thoughts was one of them.

"I didn't think anything. I was working."

"Bullshit. I was working, too, but I took one look at you in your shirt and sexy heels and all I could think about was what those long legs were gonna feel like wrapped around my back."

"So you thought I was easy upon first glance?"

"No, Doll. I saw a beautiful, sexy woman and knew I was gonna do what I could to get in there. And when you threw me attitude, I knew a hundred percent I was getting in there."

"That's easy." I pointed out.

"Again, nothing easy about you, Doll. You are the very definition of *not* easy. And straight out, just so know what happened in the shower, it's gonna happen again. Only it's gonna happen with you in a bed where I can take my time."

No. No it wasn't. I'd already embarrassed myself enough. The guys heard. Declan had shared what he'd heard with Zane, so now he knew, too. I was embarrassing myself. I was behaving like a floozy. I had a job to do, employment I was now questioning, and revenge to enact. Nowhere in there did I have time to complicate my life with great sex. And it was great. I figured if sex in the shower with Brooks standing up was great, sex in a bed where he could take his time would be even better. Off the charts better. So, no, we weren't doing it again.

"That's not going to happen. I told you already, I don't want the complication. I let myself get caught up in the moment once. I won't do it again."

"We'll see."

"Yeah, we will. And we'll see, it won't be happening again."

"Did you miss the part where I told you, a man sees something he wants he doesn't delay?"

"No."

"Right. I also told you you were the opposite of easy. Which I have to tell you, works for me. I don't like easy. I've had easy. And, Doll, it isn't all that great. Lucky for you, I like a challenge. You telling me what we shared in the shower isn't going to happen again is like waving a red flag in front of a bull. So, I'll repeat, we'll see."

Maybe I was going about this all wrong. Now that he told me he didn't like easy, I needed to change up tactics.

"I see you're workin' something out in that smart little head of yours. Just so we're clear, you coming on to me now will not be a turn-off, either."

Damn. I had nothing else to say, so I muttered, "You're annoying." I heard him chuckle and it was a nice sound. Deep and rumbly. I liked it. Maybe too much, so I continued, "And you're egotistical." His chuckle turned into a full body laugh and I forgot what we were talking about. It was so good I let it wrap around me and soak in. Mistake. Big fucking mistake. I was going to let it happen again. Double damn.

"Time for bed, Doll, I'm fuckin' wiped."

"Sounds good. I'll just go out to the—"

My words were cut off when he twisted us. He was back on his side, my back was pressed against his front, he curved back around me, and tangled his legs with mine.

"Night, Doll."

"I think—"

"Go to sleep."

"No, really, I think—"

"Sleep, Tatiana."

"Fine. But I want you to know I'm not fucking happy about the sleeping arrangements."

His body shook and I knew he was laughing at me again. Asshole.

"Noted."

Bigger asshole.

I laid there not knowing where to put my hands, with one of his under my head and the other a tight band around my stomach. Anywhere I rested mine would touch him.

"Relax, Doll. We have a long day tomorrow."

"How can I relax when you're touching me?"

He had no such trouble figuring out where he wanted my hands. He moved his from around my waist grabbed both of my hands, threaded his fingers with one of mine and held them to my chest. Shit. My ex didn't like to cuddle. Even after sex. When he was done, he was done. He rolled off, moved to his side of the bed, and went to sleep. We had a king-sized bed for a reason, he liked his space. Not even in the middle of the night did he turn closer to me. There was an invisible line down the middle. He had his side, I had mine. He never wrapped himself around me. Never held my hand, or pinned them to my chest while his thumb grazed my skin. Never. Not once. Not even when he was working to make me his. This was a problem. A huge problem. I didn't know I liked to cuddle until that very moment. And now that I knew, I was screwed.

"Relax, Tatiana."

His mouth was at my ear, and I felt more than I heard his words. And what I felt was a zap to my girly-parts. See? Totally screwed.

CHAPTER 16

This was new.

Waking up with an arm full of soft woman was not how I usually woke up. I buried my nose in unruly curls and inhaled. Though it should've been impossible, she smelled like flowers. Some sort of purpley smell that I could get used to waking up next to. On that thought, I couldn't help but to smile at how pissed she was when I crawled into bed next to her. Which of course led me to think about how even more pissed she was going to be when she woke up still in my arms.

I'd heard the guys moving around the house for the last hour, but nothing short of an RPG taking out the side of the house was going to pull me from this bed. Or from her. We had some unfinished business from last night. And I planned on doing exactly what I told her I was going to do. However, before I started I needed her fully awake and alert.

It took a while but she finally stirred. "Mornin', Doll."

Her body went from pliant and soft to stiff. And it happened immediately.

"Brooks..."

It was a clear warning to stop my roaming hands. One I was going to ignore. I pressed her closer to me and whispered, "How'd you sleep?"

"Not well," she mumbled.

"Liar."

"We need to get up."

No, we didn't. Not until I reminded her of a few things.

"Not yet." My hand moved from her stomach to her hip. And I held her where I wanted her. Her ass flush against my hard-on. "We've got time."

She didn't make me wait long, her sweet ass pushed back and my hand was on the move again. Under the elastic of her shorts, finally reaching bare skin. So fucking silky-soft, my cock jerked in response. I wanted this time to be slow. I wanted to take my time and tease her. But with her ass rubbing against my crotch it was too much. I started to push her shorts down, needing them out of my way. Thankfully she lifted her ass and took over.

"Turn your head, Doll, I want your mouth."

Without hesitation she brought her mouth to mine. So fucking sweet. Her tongue glided against mine and she moaned. That was sweet, too. Swallowing the sexy mews she made. I hitched her leg over my hip, walked my fingertips down her inner thigh, and traced along the side of her panties.

"Brooks." She broke the kiss.

"Right here, Doll."

"Please touch me."

My finger drifted over her cotton-covered slit and it was my turn to moan.

"You're soaked." I could feel her excitement through the wet material, which ratcheted up my desire.

She didn't answer. Instead, she pushed back, rubbing her bare ass against my now throbbing cock. I pushed her panties aside debating whether or not to rip the offending material clean off her body. But when my fingers touched the smooth skin of her pussy, all thoughts about underwear flew out the window. So did any thoughts of going slow.

"Keep your legs wide for me, Doll." She adjusted her leg over my hip, opening herself further. Two fingers slipped in and she bucked. "So fucking hot and wet."

And I did what I'd told her I'd do last night, I didn't delay. With my fingers working her pussy, my other hand went under her shirt, yanked the cup of her bra down, and palmed her perky tit. I was mindless, my hands moved on their own, purely on instinct. I pinched and rolled her nipple while I made sure the heel of my hand was grinding down on her clit as my fingers worked in and out of her tight slit.

"Brooks," she panted.

I'd planned on only getting her off with my fingers, but the need in her voice was my undoing.

I yanked my hand out of her panties, rolled her to her back, pushed her shirt up, bra down, and finally tugged her underwear down her legs, tossing them over my shoulder. I barely had my cock freed when she wrapped her long legs around my hips and tightened them. I palmed my hard-on and guided the tip inside, and with one hard thrust I buried myself deep.

Fuck.

Better than I remembered.

Fucking fantastic.

Tatiana squeezed her thighs around me and threw her head back.

"Yes."

I lowered myself over her, rested on my forearm. I drove in hard. One hand went between us and I knew I found what I was looking for when her hips jerked and she groaned. I set a brutal pace and let myself go. Her hands pawed at my back and she held on with her legs, meeting me thrust for thrust.

"Mouth, babe. I wanna taste your moans as you come around my cock."

She righted her head, but instead of kissing her like I told her I wanted, I couldn't tear my eyes away from hers. Soft. Heated. Needful. Just like I'd seen the first time. So fucking beautiful that if I'd had any control left it was gone.

"Get there, Tatiana," I begged.

Pleasure surrounded me, tingling had started at the base of my spine and it'd spread everywhere. My balls were tightening and threatening to explode. Her inner muscles spasmed and I was losing the battle. She was too tight. Too hot. Too sexy. Too fucking much, I couldn't handle it. She was staring right back into my eyes and just like all the times before they were telling me everything.

"Baby," I panted in warning. "I'm gonna come. Catch up."

I was so damn lost in everything that was Tatiana Jones I feared I'd be lost forever.

"Brooks," she wailed and I slammed my mouth onto hers. With one last thrust I fell. The taste of her enveloped me, her pussy convulsed, her legs around my back twitched, her arms around my neck tightened. Yeah, I was lost in her. And I was more than all right with it.

I slowed our kiss, not wanting it to end. I knew the minute our lips pulled apart she'd close down. I wasn't ready for the bullshit she was going to say. The lies she was going to try to convince herself of. I didn't want to see the shine in her pretty eyes turn hard. Not after what we just shared. The sex was great, better than great, but it was the look she'd given me that was better. No pretense. No bullshit. No hiding. In the time she'd held my gaze and allowed me to see her, the real unguarded her, meant something to me. And what it meant was, shit had just changed between us.

Knowing what I knew about Monroe and how he'd dicked her over, yet she still gave me that. Yeah, shit had changed. And I was not a stupid man, I wouldn't squander what she'd given me. Even if she wasn't aware she had.

"Mornin'," I repeated, moving my lips from hers to the soft skin of her neck.

"Morning," she returned, stretching, giving me better access to her throat.

"You taste so fucking good." My tongue traced her jaw up to her ear. "So damn sweet," I whispered when I made it to her ear.

Thank God, my softening dick was still inside of her or I would've missed how her insides clenched at my admission. I'd thought her eyes told the real story, but I'd found another way to figure out what she liked. She could lie with her words, but her body would tell the truth. That meant good things for me. I planned on spending a considerable amount of time inside of her.

"So do you." I lifted my head in shock and stared down at her. Still soft and relaxed. "What?"

"Nothing. Sometimes you surprise me." Her brows pulled together and I used my thumb to smooth the furrowed skin. "You ready for breakfast?"

Gone was the lazy sated look. "Yeah."

"No way, Tatiana. Don't put that hand back up."

"I'm—"

"Yes, you are. You're getting ready to close up and kick me out of this bed. I'm telling you now, that's not gonna happen. Yesterday, I fucked up and walked outta the shower when I should've stayed and set you straight."

"Set me straight?" The creases on her forehead were back, this time no amount of smoothing was going to work to flatten the skin.

"That's what I said."

"I heard what you said, Brooks. I'm just a little surprised you think you can straighten me out."

"Doll."

"Don't 'Doll' me. And you're right, I'm kicking you out of bed. Get off me."

Her legs unwrapped from around my hips, she planted them on the bed, and she jerked her hips up.

Bad play. When she pulled her bottom lip into her mouth and bit down, I knew she'd found the error in her movement. With my cock still buried inside of her, she'd done nothing but drive me deeper.

"Tatiana," I warned. "Stay still."

Her eyes snapped to mine and they were shooting fire. Passion and anger swirled together.

"Get up." She bucked again.

"Baby, you keep movin' like that, he's gonna get up. And when he does, we're going for round two."

"Not gonna happen, Brooks."

"Heard that before, Doll. Considering my dick is still inside of you and getting harder by the second I think I proved it's gonna happen."

"You're annoying," she moaned.

"No. I'm right."

And once again, the words she spoke were bullshit but her body wasn't lying. Neither were her eyes. Sharp fingernails blazed a path up my back and I wondered if she'd drawn blood as they made their way into my hair. With two handfuls, she pulled my head down and met me halfway. Her kiss was desperate, hungry, but no less sweet. Her hips bucked again and even though I'd come a few minutes before, I was ready again.

"Roll over," she murmured on my lips.

With a shake of my head, I denied her request and slammed into her. Over and over I thrusted harder, faster. I couldn't deny what our bodies wanted.

"Roll over," she repeated on a groan. Her hips bucking harder this time. I gave in and took her with me as I settled on my back.

Why the fuck had I denied her first demand? She looked magnificent perched on my lap. Full tits on display, flat stomach, strong thighs pressed against mine, the muscles straining as she lifted herself up and then lowered down on my dick. Christ, she was the sexiest thing I'd ever seen.

"Baby, lean forward." She ignored me and slammed down, rocking her hips and grinding before she lifted up again. "Tatiana. Lean down."

She wasn't paying attention to a damn thing I was saying. She didn't slow, didn't acknowledge me, didn't even look at me. She was lost in her own world as she fucked the hell out of me. Everything about her felt good, except the no eye contact. I quickly knifed up and fisted her hair, bringing her face close to mine.

"When you're fucking me, you look at me. You do not go inside your head," I growled. Her eyes blinked and she finally focused on me. "There you are. When I'm inside of you, I get all of you. Your eyes are on me. You do not ever go someplace else."

She nodded and I laid back down, bringing her with me.

"Ride me, baby. But keep your pretty eyes open and look at me. I wanna watch you fall apart." Her head bobbed her response and her hips rocked. "Good God, you feel good. So fucking beautiful." Our gazes locked and I watched as an emotion I couldn't read took over.

Tatiana was rough, she was wild, and she could fuck. It took her minutes to take me to the edge.

"Come on, baby, get there. I'm close."

My hands left her ass and cupped both of her tits, bringing one to my mouth I latched on and rolled my tongue around the hard nipple. My confession had her grinding harder, moving faster, if she didn't catch up I was going to come without her. Finally her body shook and she flew apart. I'd forgotten all about my own pleasure, watching her take hers. I felt the pressure building, I was vaguely aware my cock was jerking and my orgasm had broken loose. But none of that mattered. Watching Tatiana quiver in ecstasy was better.

I was beyond physical attraction, we'd slid firmly into complicated.

CHAPTER 17

Brooks made me lose my mind. Totally and completely. Not only had it taken him less than five seconds and only one squeeze on my hip to have me pushing my ass into him like a hussy in heat, but I was quick to jump at a chance for seconds. What the hell was wrong with me? And he'd gotten extremely growly and bossy. Instead of telling him to take a long walk off a short pier, my body electrified and obeyed. My eyes had snapped to his and he'd pulled me out of my dark thoughts. I'd demanded he let me ride him, but once I was on top, panic took over. I was on full display. He could see my scars. I had to look away, I couldn't bear to see the look of disgust on his face. What if he saw them and he—

"Tatiana," Brooks snapped.

"Huh?"

My vision cleared and I realized I was still on top of him. And man-oh-man he looked angry. Not a look one would expect from a man who had just had two orgasms. Thank God, I was leaning forward with my boobs mostly smashed against his very hard, very fine chest. This time around, I hadn't missed how strong and well-defined every muscle was. But right then, I wasn't concentrating on his muscle definition. I was in a pickle. How in the hell was I going to get off of Brooks without allowing him to see me?

"Baby." He swept my hair away from my face and over my shoulder. "You keep zoning out on me."

"I'm just tired."

"Bullshit."

"Stop doing that. You don't know what I'm thinking."

"Yeah, Doll, I do. And it's bullshit." No longer caring, since I was pissed, I made my move and tried to roll off of him. "Not gonna happen."

"What's not?"

"The hand. You closing down and pushing me away. You telling yourself a bunch of fucked-up lies. None of it."

"The only thing I've lied to myself about is, thinkin' this was a good idea," I returned.

I had nowhere to go. One arm was like a steel band around my back holding me in place, the other was shoved in my hair and he was holding on there, too. I couldn't move. Well, I could, but not without a struggle, and that struggle would result in him seeing me.

"No, baby, this being a *good* idea, is the only thing that's *not* fucked-up."

"You're pissing me off," I warned.

"You were pissed off a mile back. I'm okay with you

being pissed. What I'm not okay with is you filling your head with a bunch of garbage. You are beautiful."

If I could've covered my ears like a petulant child, I would've. I didn't want to hear his shit. There was nothing beautiful about me. Nothing. He didn't need to sweet talk me to get me into bed with him. I'd already proved I was a sure thing, times three.

"Let go of me."

"Not until you listen."

"Just stop. Please."

"No way am I going to let you ruin what we just shared. When you forget and lose yourself you are a sight. You are wild and free."

"I'm not wild," I protested.

"Baby, you are. You gave yourself to me and I'm not letting you take it back."

"I didn't give myself to you."

I was arguing just to argue. I needed to find a way to get away from him and out of the bed. His tone was far too possessive. The last thing I needed was the entanglement. The way he looked at me, touched me, held me close to him all night was too much. I couldn't get lost in him, we had a job to do. When it was over, we'd both walk away. I didn't need a broken heart when that happened.

"I think the last hour proves you wrong."

"We need to get up."

"We will, in a minute."

"What are you waiting for?"

"A good morning kiss."

"Oh, no. No more kissing. No more touching. No more sleeping in the same bed. I'll take the couch."

I was a little afraid of the lazy smile that played on his lips. I didn't need him to utter the words to know he didn't agree with my moratorium.

"Stop fucking around and kiss me good morning."

"Not gonna happen, Brooks. We need to get up. I have work to do. I have to go to the naval base and drop off some documents before we leave Bahrain."

"Then you better hurry, Doll."

Why wasn't I wrestling out of his grasp? I could've easily fought his hold and broken free. But I wasn't. I was still perched on his lap, naked, with his dick pressed between us. Why did he have to be so damn sexy? Or maybe a better question was, why was I so fucking weak?

All it took was the slightest bit of pressure on the back of my head and I was lowering my lips to his. He wasn't smug about my acquiescence. As a matter of fact, when his eyes locked onto mine they gentled. He looked almost proud. Maybe I was seeing things and he was simply amused he was getting his way—again.

He didn't allow me to kiss him, like he'd asked. As soon as my lips touched his, he halted my progress. Instead of allowing me to take control, he slowly grazed his lips against mine. Feather soft. His stubble a barely-there scrape as he kissed the corner of my mouth.

"You are so beautiful."

He placed another peck square on my mouth.

"Absolutely perfect."

He moved to the other side and another brush of his lips.

"I can't get enough of you."

My heart pounded, my legs trembled, and my hands

on his chest shook. He had to stop talking. I pressed in closer and swept my tongue across his lips, preventing him from saying anything else.

"Goddamn, never been kissed like that before, Doll. I could spend all day in this bed with you doing nothing but exploring that sexy as fuck mouth of yours."

The kissing, touching, and sex was less potent than his words. When he said those things to me, he made me want to believe. I wanted to be beautiful. But I wasn't. I was anything but perfect. My flesh was marred and mangled. Brooks was out of my league. Out in the real world, he could have any number of sexy women at his beck and call. I was a convenient lay while he was out on an op.

“One of these days, you'll believe me, that the shit you allow to swirl in your head is utter shit.” I hated that he could read me so easily. "Up you go."

"Um... Maybe..."

"Not a goddamn chance you're trying to roll off me so you can hide. This is day one of me washing that shit from your head. There is not one thing about you I don't find beautiful."

"Brooks." I snapped. "Stop saying that crap. We both know it's not true."

I found myself flying through the air, flat on my back, and Brooks’ large frame looming over me before I knew what was going on. "You calling me a liar, Tatiana?"

"No. Not a liar. I think you're trying to be polite."

"Doll, we've been over this. I don't say shit just to say it. I'm not polite, I'm honest."

He sat up and rearranged my legs so they were

wrapped around his back and he stared down at me. With one hand still on my hip, his other traced the puckered scars on my stomach.

"Please, don't."

He ignored me and continued, touching each one of them. Tenderly. I couldn't stand to watch, to feel his roughened fingertips lightly caress my disgusting skin.

"Stop, Brooks."

His exploration progressed but his gaze came to me. Brooks' eyes held mine and his hand roamed. I felt the stinging and the liquid was nearly brimming over. I could do nothing to stop the tears from rolling down my cheeks.

"Damn you," I hissed. "Stop."

"Each and every one of these marks represents how strong you are. How mentally tough you are. What your body can endure because you are fierce. Each scar a reminder that you are a force to be reckoned with. Your determination, will, how capable you are. Every blemish tells a story of survival and courage. You are goddamn beautiful and it has nothing to do with your pretty face, soft hair, great fucking legs, and everything to do with these." His big hand spanned my stomach, almost covering all of the pockmarks. "Your strength makes you the most beautiful woman I've ever seen. And mark this, Tatiana, one day you're gonna see what I see. But in the meantime, I'm gonna remind you and I'm gonna do it often. No way in hell should a woman like you live her life hiding away with a hand up. That hand is gonna fall, too. And when it does, I'll prove to you where you land is a safe and good place to be."

When Brooks stopped speaking, I had no choice but to come to the realization I wasn't walking away with my heart intact. When he left, I'd have a Brooks Miller-sized hole in my chest. And I would bet it was going to hurt worse than any beating I'd received while in enemy hands.

CHAPTER 18

By the time I'd allowed Tatiana out of bed, the guys were done with breakfast and were sitting around the table going over the latest information Tex and Garrett, our in-house intel specialist, had sent over. No one said a word about me missing breakfast, and when Tatiana joined us a few minutes later no one said anything to her, either. Which was good because I was still mad as hell the woman disappeared into her head and believed she was somehow damaged and disgusting. It gutted me she thought so little of herself. If nothing else, by the end of this mission, she'd see herself how I did. Capable and strong.

"What time are we leaving?" Tatiana asked, as she poured herself a cup of coffee.

"Twenty hundred. It's a six-hour drive to the eastern province," Declan answered.

"I have to drop off some documents at the naval base and send a few emails before we leave. Leon instructed me to send the UN my resignation effective immediately," she told us.

She'd told me about needing to go to base, but not quitting her job.

"Why does he want you to quit?" I asked.

"For one, the parameters of my job with the UN are based exclusively in Bahrain. The other issue is, Z Corps will be taking over my salary."

"What did Z tell you about The Company?" Kyle inquired.

"Not a lot. He said he knew more than me, but not as much as he would've liked to know. He also shared he had unease but didn't elaborate. I don't know Zane as well as the rest of you but I do know he's not a liar. If he has concerns, then I need to consider what that means for me."

I found it interesting she was giving care to what Z had told her. She was correct about one thing, Z didn't bullshit. He was as straight as they came. If he said she needed to be mindful and watch her back, then she needed to be careful.

"What do you know about this Leon Brown?" I asked.

"Just what I told you. The name is obviously an alias. He gives me orders, I follow them. My after-action reports and SITREPS are verbally given directly to him. I have zero contact with anyone else."

"You trust him?" I continued to pry.

"As much as I can trust anyone."

That was a CIA bullshit answer. There was very little trust among spies. They all knew the agency could and would turn against them. Even their fellow operatives would slit your throat if they were ordered to.

"Let me ask you another way, do you trust him with your life?"

"I have for the past couple of years."

"Wrong answer."

"What do you mean, wrong answer? Considering he's the only one who knows my mission specifics, I've obviously trusted him with my life."

"If you were to ask me if I trust any of these men." I swept the room with my hand. "With my life my answer would be, yes. Just, yes. Emphatically, yes. No hesitation. I would trust them with your life. No question. There is reluctance in your eyes. I don't like doubt, especially when we're talking about my ass swinging in the wind if you do not a hundred percent trust Leon Brown."

"I wouldn't trust him with your life," she admitted.

"I'll call Z while you two are delivering her documents to the base and see what he says about giving Leon limited intel," Declan told us. "Just to add, Tatiana, if you don't trust him to have our six, you shouldn't trust him with yours. I'll see if Z has anything new on The Company. He hates the unknown. I'd bet he's been all over Garrett's ass to find anything and everything."

"I appreciate you asking Zane, but I can go to the base by myself. There's no need to inconvenience anyone."

"No-go, Doll. I'm taggin' along," I told her.

"Why? That's stupid. I've traveled all over Bahrain by myself, Brooks. I don't need an escort."

I was trying to hold back my amusement. She was

feisty when she was annoyed. Not only was it cute as hell, it turned me on like nobody's business.

"Didn't think you did."

She sipped her coffee and glared at me. I assumed she was waiting for me to tell her I'd stay behind. That wasn't happening. I didn't care how many times she'd gallivanted around the country by herself, shit had changed. One of the changes was someone was actively trying to kill her. Another was she now had me as a shadow. I didn't give two fucks if it made her mad.

"But you're still coming with me, aren't you?" She set her coffee down on the countertop.

"Yep."

"Why are you so hard-headed? Seriously, you have your own shit to do. The little woman doesn't need a big strong man to follow her around."

"Careful, babe, that giant chip on your shoulder is showing."

"Whatever, asshole. I don't want you coming. Besides, you don't have clearance to get where I'm going."

"Didn't ask if you wanted me to come. Unlike what you are used to, none of us go out alone. We always have someone at our back. Safety in numbers and all that good shit."

"Right, so I guess when you told me you went out to scout out the Bitoo brothers' location, one of the guys went with you?" She grinned.

"There's always a special exception."

"Great. So, make one now."

"The two of you gonna stand around and bitch all day? As amusing as it is watching Brooks chase his tail, we all got shit to do." Thad chuckled. "And I think it is worth repeating, it is amusing."

Tatiana's face paled when she remembered we had an audience. Her pretty eyes narrowed and I lost the battle. What had started off as a snicker was soon a full-blown belly laugh.

Her eyes rolled and I would swear on a stack of bibles I could hear her teeth grinding.

"You hungry, Doll? I can make us something to eat before we head out."

I wanted to remind her she'd burned a hell of a lot of calories this morning, but I held my tongue. I liked her sassy and annoyed, not embarrassed and ashamed. The way her cheeks tinted pink, it seemed she didn't need the prompt.

"I'm not hungry."

"Then I'm ready when you are."

"I'll grab my stuff." Wisely, she didn't try to argue further.

I waited until she was in the bedroom before I sorted through the papers on the table. "Anything new I need to know?"

"Falcon Holdings has proved to be a gold mine. Tex is connecting dots left and right. Taking out Al Issa is priority number one. If we can recover any of the artifacts, that's gravy, but not our first concern," Dec told me.

"What else has Tex found?"

"Falcon Holdings owns other companies' outstanding stocks. When Tex looked into the companies, most of them are bogus. Nothing produced, no goods sold, nothing purchased. Those are the companies he's focusing on. He even found one that traces back to dog rings and cockfighting. It seems that South America has a huge issue with it," Max added.

"Why would that even be on Tex's radar?"

"Because it pulls in millions of dollars, and why are people investing big money into a fake corporation that's only income source is animal blood sports?" Max's brow lifted.

His question was rhetorical and didn't require an answer, but I had a question. "Seriously?"

"Serious as a heart attack."

"Well, damn. I thought dogfighting was low-end bullshit. Street gangs and thugs. I had no idea it was that lucrative."

"Brother, big time players are involved. Tex is confident he can track it back to Omni."

"Track what back?" Tatiana asked, coming back into the dining room with her backpack over her shoulder.

"Cocks." I wagged my eyebrows.

"Are you thirteen?" She glared.

“No, really, we're talking about cockfighting in South America.”

“Actually, we were talking about the money involved in dog fighting,” Max interjected.

“Oh, yeah, it’s huge. I know a woman back in San Diego, Faith, who works in a shelter who saves pit bulls. It’s dangerous going in and trying to get the dogs. There’s a lot of money being thrown around, and that’s on the low scale,” she told us. “Anything new with Al Issa?”

“Tex’s latest intel shows Al Issa at his palace. The full

staff and extra guards indicates he's gonna be there awhile."

"Are we taking out the compound or waiting for him to be on the move, with less security?" Tatiana questioned.

"Right now, the plan is to take the compound. That's our best shot at recovering the missing tablets," Declan relayed. Tatiana continued to study the satellite images Tex had sent over. "What are you thinking?"

"I think that's a lot of armed guards. I count ten on the perimeter. Three in the courtyard. Five on the roof. Not to mention, he'll have a personal detail surrounding him. That's eighteen guns we can see, and more than likely a shit ton we can't. There are six of us." She told us something we'd already calculated.

"Easy day," I told her.

"I hate that SEAL shit. All your tough-guy lingo doesn't make you invincible. We'll be out-numbered a minimum of three to one. His staff will be armed, too. Not to mention, the sympathizers in the area will come to his aid. Al Issa isn't stupid. He keeps the locals in money, just for this reason."

Max, Thad, Kyle, and Declan all chuckled at her outburst. Obviously she wasn't pleased they'd found humor in aggravation. She looked madder than a wet hen.

"We'll set charges in the surrounding area as a distraction. Once those go off, we'll set the perimeter to blow—"

"Or, you wait until he leaves the compound and take out his convoy. The guards will scramble to the location, leaving minimal security at the compound and I can slip in and snatch the tablets."

"Doll, this isn't a quick snatch and grab. And once

again, there's not a snowball's chance in hell you're going anywhere alone," I corrected.

"That's—"

"Not up for negotiation," Declan cut her off. "Once we have updated intel, we'll go over mission specifics. Until then, wrap up your business in Bahrain so we can get ready to go."

Tatiana looked like she wanted to argue but wisely kept quiet. I understood she'd spent the last two years working on her own, but she was going to have to learn that no man on the team was ever going to let her go into a situation solo. That wasn't how we worked. Every man had a battle buddy. It was smart—two is one, one is none.

"You ready?" I asked.

"Yep."

Her short-clipped answer made me smile. Hot damn, she was feisty. And so pretty even in her cargos and long-sleeved button-up shirt that showed none of her toned, tanned flesh. I didn't need to see it, the memory of her hot and sweaty on top of me was tattooed on my soul.

CHAPTER 19

The first ten minutes of our drive was done in silence. I was more annoyed than I should've been but after the morning I'd had, my nerves were fried. I couldn't remember a better way to wake up than in Brooks' strong arms. And the two smokin' hot rounds of toe-curling sex were fantastic, too. It was the vulnerability I could've gone without. The verbal sparring where Brooks had outright told me he thought I was beautiful. I still didn't believe him but when he'd promised to make me see what he saw, I wanted to. I wanted to feel as strong and as brave as he thought I was. I knew I was more than capable of doing my job, but I no longer felt courageous.

"We have a tail," Brooks told me, breaking the silence.

"White Mercedes?" I asked.

"Yep."

I'd been watching the car in the side mirror for the last few miles. The driver was trying to stay a few lengths back but he stupidly changed lanes every time Brooks had.

"Where are you going to try and ditch him?"

"Once we get closer to the naval base. On the north side, near the pedestrian entrance."

"There's nothing there but small side streets. Most are one-way. I think you should stay on the Causeway, take the last exit before the bridge. To the east of the base, there's nothing but industrial parks, it will be safer without the congestion of all the shops on the north side."

"I agree less traffic, but a wide-open space gives him a better opportunity to catch up. Not to mention, a straight shot if he opens fire."

"Ah. I hadn't realized Brooks Miller was afraid of a little gun play."

"Being shot at is not my most favorite pastime. I'm more concerned about what the passenger's packing. I'd prefer not to give them the range to detonate an RPG."

That was my preference as well. I'd had enough of having missiles shot at me for a lifetime.

"Take us into the industrial park. Better to be on the offensive."

"And what? You gonna go all Wile E. Coyote? Did I miss where you packed your dynamite and boomerang?"

I would've been pissed if it wasn't for Brooks' playful tone. Something strange hit my chest, normally when I picked up a tail, adrenaline kicked in and I got a little nervous. I was always by myself. I had no one to rely on but me. But today I had Brooks, and in turn, he had me. The heart-pounding fear of someone hunting me was absent. Together, Brooks and I would figure something out.

"You totally missed me packin' the car. I have my Wonder Woman Underoos on under my cargos, too."

"Goddamn, Doll," he choked out. "You cannot tell me shit that is going to make my dick hard while some asshole is following us."

His comment made me smile. "I can't? Why not?"

Brooks gave me a sideways glance as he weaved in and out of traffic, putting more space between us and the Mercedes.

"They're not gonna wait until we get to the exit." All the humor in Brooks' voice was gone. "Passenger's making a move."

I unbuckled my seat belt and started for the back seat when Brooks' hand on my bicep halted my progress. "What are you doing? Put your belt back on and get down," he snapped.

With a shrug I knocked his hand away and found what I was looking for. Out the back windshield I could see the passenger of the Mercedes, now sitting on the open window frame.

"He's gonna take his shot, Brooks," I warned.

Sure enough, the man fired through the traffic-laden Causeway. His shot went wide and came nowhere near our car. But the surrounding drivers quickly sped up or pulled to the side of the road, giving the shooter his desired outcome, a clear shot.

"Goddammit, Tatiana. Get a fucking seat belt on now!" Brooks yelled.

"Hold your underwear on, jeeze."

With the AR15 now in my hand I'd almost righted myself back into my seat when Brooks veered hard right, making my body thrash.

"Seat. Belt!" he growled again.

“Oh, for fuck’s sake. I'm not putting the damn belt back on and sitting here like some helpless ninny.” I quickly checked the magazine was full, pulled the charging handle, lowered the passenger window, and facing rear, I balanced on my knees. “Your choice, brake and get me a shot of the fucker shooting at us or switch lanes and get me in view of the driver.”

“Christ,” he mumbled, looking in the rearview mirror. “The driver will be easier. Brace yourself.”

I flipped up the rubber lens covers on the Aimpoint CompM4 Red Dot sight, steadied myself the best I could, and shouldered the AR15. Brooks switched lanes and hit the brakes. I took aim, clicked the safety off, and waited for a clear shot.

I had the driver in my sights “In three…two…” I pressed the trigger.

Three things happened at once; the recoil of the rifle and the awkwardness of shooting left-handed out of a moving vehicle made me flinch, my ears hurt so fucking bad from the .223 being fired in a small space with no ear-pro in, and the driver of the white Mercedes slumped.

“Goddamn, woman.”

I could barely hear Brooks over the ringing in my ears. I recapped the Aimpoint, ejected the round from the chamber, and clicked the lever back to safe, keeping the AR in the front seat with me.

“I think I busted my eardrums,” I told him as I sat

down in the seat. "Thank God, I only needed one shot or my ears would be bleeding."

"Now that you've taken care of that issue, how 'bout we get back to the Underoo conversation?"

"Are you always like this?"

"Like what?"

"Have sex-brain in the middle of car chases?"

As soon as the question rolled off my tongue, I realized I didn't want to know the answer. Mainly because it would crush me if he said yes, but also, I didn't want to know anything about Brooks' past. The less I knew about him, the easier it would be when he walked away.

"Hell, no. The guys on my team don't talk about their underwear. And if they wear Wonder Woman Underoos I don't wanna know."

With a sharp nod I continued to stare out the windshield.

"Doll." He reached for my hand and intertwined our fingers. "The answer is still hell no, however I'll clarify. I have never found a woman wearing cargos, tac vest, and brain bucket sexy—until you. I have never, not once, gotten a hard-on when a teammate, male or female, was checkin' the magazines and rackin' the slide of their firearms—until you. I have never taken a shower or crawled into bed with a woman while on an op. I've certainly never had sex on a mission. And I've never thought about the sexy woman next me's panties while she was expertly handling an assault rifle out the window of a moving car. Does that answer your question?"

I swallowed the lump in my throat and gave the only answer I could manage. "Yep."

"Good."

My mind was racing a mile a minute trying to digest what Brooks had told me. More information I didn't want to process. It was my fault, I'd stupidly asked. I was getting too wrapped up in what he thought of me and how he saw me. Then savoring the feeling his words invoked. I foolishly wanted to believe him when he called me sexy and beautiful. I hadn't felt those things for a long time, and I never thought I'd feel them again. It shouldn't matter to me how I looked or what others saw, but it did.

"Don't you need to call the team and tell them what happened?" I asked.

"No need. Thad and Kyle were a few cars behind the Mercedes."

"Seriously?"

"I keep telling you, we always have backup. You think that when I tell you you're not going somewhere alone, it's because you're a woman. It has nothing to do with your gender and everything to do with being a part of a team."

"Well, who has Thad and Kyle's back?"

"Us."

I'd never been a part of a team. When I was in the CIA, I had a partner and I'd worked with others but I'd never felt like I was truly a part of a crew. There was comradery but no real loyalty. I needed to be careful. A girl could get used to this.

CHAPTER 20

Once again, I was thoroughly impressed with Tatiana. Nothing seemed to frazzle her. Except me. And if I was being honest with myself, I liked that—a fuck of a lot. During the incident with the Merc on the Causeway, she hadn't broken a sweat. When we got to base, she was cool, collected, and professional when she met with the UN liaison. No one would've guessed thirty minutes prior she'd been shot at and returned fire from a moving vehicle. Not to mention, Kyle had called in and confirmed she'd killed the driver. The news hadn't seemed to bother her one bit. Her only comment when I told her she'd hit the man in the throat was, she was disappointed with her aim. She intended on a head shot. The team was fast learning she was a valuable addition.

However, when we were alone, I saw a whole different side of her. She couldn't hide her vulnerability. Her unsure, soft side shone through like a beacon. A softness I wanted to protect and self-esteem I wanted to help her rebuild. And when she was in my arms and let go, the gift of her was so promising, I knew I was in trouble. She'd been in my bed a total of one night and I was already trying to figure out a way to make her stay. The situation was messy and problematic. Zane was going to have a shit hemorrhage. Not that I gave the first fuck, after he chewed my ass, he'd deal. After all, it wasn't like I was the first man on his team to complicate shit. Hell, Jasmin and Linc were married and on the same team. If they could figure it out, there was no doubt I could. Not that I was thinking about marriage. That would've been downright insane. But I wasn't letting her kick me out of our bed anytime soon.

"Yo." Max poked his head in my room, pulling me from my thoughts. "Garrett's on the phone. He's got intel on the guys from today."

I zipped my backpack and answered, "Perfect timing. Just finished packing up."

I followed Max into the dining room and looked around. All the maps and SITREPS had been cleared off the table in preparation for our departure. I checked my watch, noting we had less than a half hour until we needed to be on the road.

"Zane crackin' the whip, or what? It's the middle of the night. What are you doing in the office?" I asked Garrett.

"Thad sent over the fingerprints from the driver he scanned. Since he couldn't pull anything from the passenger, I only have half the intel I would like. But I hit pay dirt with the driver."

After Tatiana shot the driver, the Mercedes careened into a cement barrier. The passenger that had been sitting in the window firing at us was mangled beyond recognition and Thad and Kyle hadn't been able to pull prints or get a useable photo for facial identification.

"What'd you find?" Declan asked.

"The driver, Kyril Rahal, is a known associate of Matek Nazari. It seems Nazari put a hefty price on Tatiana's head. He believes she has the four Cuneiform tablets."

"Did he take out the Bitoo brothers?"

"Doubtful. The Bitoos were fucked for a variety of reasons, but Nazari thinks Tatiana has the tablets. He'd have no reason to go after the brothers. The prince would, though. He knew they went outside of the auction and was working with an American to sell them."

"You think Al Issa has the tablets now?"

"If the Bitoos were stupid enough to keep them in the warehouse. And evidence suggests they're dumber than they looked, so yeah, I think Al Issa took out the brothers and took his tablets back."

Declan continued to pepper Garrett with questions, however I was still stuck on Nazari putting another hit out on Tatiana. I wanted to know more about that.

"What about the price Nazari put out for Tatiana?" I asked.

"I was getting to that," Garrett told me. "Z thinks the easiest way to shut Matek Nazari down is by doing it permanently. I tracked him to Al Qatif. You'll detour there before you continue to the Eastern Providence. Al Qatif is only a forty-five-minute drive after you cross the King Fahd bridge. I'll send you the coordinates. The only snag is his two sons and daughter are with him."

"How old are his children?" Kyle inquired.

"Adult-aged. The eldest son is twenty-five, daughter is twenty-three, youngest son is twenty-one," Tatiana answered. "And they will be an issue for us. Even the daughter. All three are heavily into his businesses."

"Do we have the green light to take out all four if necessary?" Declan asked for clarification.

"Affirmative. Scope of the mission is all four, but only if Nazari's children directly engage."

"And will they?" Thad asked Tatiana.

"If they see us, yes," she answered.

"Then we make ourselves visible," Declan said. "I don't want any loose ends following us around Saudi Arabia. Or some sort of revenge scenario a few years from now."

"Agreed," I told him. Tatiana seemed to be deep in contemplation. "What's wrong, Doll?"

"Maybe we need to reconsider me staying with the team. Nazari is after me. If I—"

"No," I cut her off.

"Zane thought you might say something like that," Garrett cut in. "He sent a message. Let me read it so I don't leave anything out. And I quote, 'Suck it up, buttercup. Being part of a team is taking care of one another. Something those CIA fucks know nothing about. You're not abandoning your team or your mission.' End quote."

"But if I—"

"Not happening," I told her.

"I could—"

"No."

"Brooks! Stop fucking interrupting me for fuck's sake, you're annoying as shit. I could head to Al Qatif by myself, handle the Nazari issue, and meet back up with you guys tomorrow. That way we're not behind schedule."

I was trying to keep my cool. But my patience was fast running out. It seemed Tatiana wanted to ditch me every chance she got. She'd already run out once and I had to damn near bribe her to get her to come back to the compound with me. This shit was getting old. Maybe I was wrong, maybe she didn't feel the same connection I felt.

"Either you're a part of the team or you're not. Your choice, Tatiana. None of us is going to beg you to stay. In or out, make a fucking decision and stick with it." Her wide eyes came to mine and they flashed something new, injury. Too damn bad, we didn't have time for bullshit, and if she took offense to me being straight with her, tough titties. "Garrett, you got anything else for us?"

"Negative. Coordinates and mission codes have been sent to all of you. Good luck, be safe, and stay dangerous." Garrett disconnected.

"We're out in five," Declan called out, as he left the room.

Max, Thad, and Kyle all followed Dec, leaving Tatiana and I alone.

"Got anything else you wanna get off your chest?" she snapped.

"You got some brass balls, that's for sure, Tatiana."

"What does that mean?"

"Trying to put your shit on me. If you're having second thoughts about being on this team, now's the time to speak up. We're getting ready to go into an uncertain situation and I need to know if you're all in. If you're not, hit the road."

"Nice."

"Nothing nice about it."

She rolled her eyes and asked, "You always act like a child when you're pissed?"

Was that what this was? Was I behaving like a pansy ass because I had a case of the feels? I wouldn't know, I'd never been in a situation like this. She was hot for me one minute, running the next. Not ever had I been so knotted up over a woman. Especially one who had ghosted me and pushed me away whenever she could.

I took the two steps needed to come face-to-face with her. She stood straighter and pushed her shoulders back readying herself for battle. "What are you so afraid of?" I asked.

"I'm not afraid." Her eyes went from mine to somewhere behind me.

"Eyes on me." It took a minute but when her gaze landed back to mine, I finished. "I know that douchebag ex of yours let you down, but I'm thinking it's more than that. Someone else fucked you over. My guess is someone you worked with in the CIA. You can deny it all you want, but you're scared as shit."

"No one let me down."

"Then why are you so afraid?"

"I told you—"

"You're lying. You keep trying to ditch us. The first time was when those idiots took a shot at us on the boat. The second is when they tried to breach the compound. And now that Nazari has sent someone else after you,

you're trying it again. Maybe you're scared *and* you don't trust us."

"Has it occurred to you that I'm trying to keep the five of you safe? Nazari is sending people to kill me. *Me*. Not any of you. However, if you're with me, there's a possibility one of you could be collateral damage."

"Not gonna happen."

"You're so smug, you think a bullet won't kill you?"

"Doll, when my time's up, it's up. I die just as easily as any other man. The difference is, Nazari ain't too smart and neither are the amateurs he's been sending in. I'm not worried because, again, he ain't too smart."

Tatiana was holding something else back. Damn stubborn woman. "Why are you scared?"

"I'm not."

"Goddamn, woman! What has you so afraid?"

I was being a dick and I knew it. Seemed the only way to make her tell the truth was when she was cornered and pissed. I wasn't proud of my behavior, nor was I ashamed. I'd do whatever it took to get her to talk.

"I don't want you to get hurt," she practically growled. "It's not you I don't trust. It's me, you asshole."

"You?"

"You didn't get yourself captured and beaten. I did. It wasn't you who fucked up and walked into a trap. It was me who did. I trusted my gut and almost got myself killed. Obviously, it's me who cannot be trusted and I don't want anyone getting hurt because my instincts suck."

"That's jacked," I told her.

"No. It's real."

"If by 'real' you mean what you've brainwashed yourself into believing."

"Brooks!"

"Doll, you know as well as I do it's a chance we all take. You strap on a vest the same as I do. We plan, we have backup plans, we go with our gut, we study the intel, and still shit can go sideways. It's the name of the game and we all play."

"I get that, Brooks. However, I walked right into it. I wanted to prove to myself that after everything that happened with James, I wasn't as inept has he told me I was. I went back to work with a fire in my belly wanting to reaffirm my competence. And what did I do? I didn't fucking listen. There were conflicting reports. I chose to follow the intel that would give me the fastest results, not what was safest or right. So, yes, I know the game, I willingly play it, but this was not an operation that went sideways. It was my fault. All of it."

"You're not the first operative to take a risk and have it be the wrong choice, and you won't be the last. We all have fire in our bellies. It's what makes us good at our jobs. We all have something to prove to ourselves. Each time we train, we push harder. Each mission we try to execute it better. We are constantly proving, pushing, improving. It is what we do. You can't beat yourself up about one fuck-up. Learn from it. Grow. Then move the fuck on. If you second-guess every decision, you'll paralyze yourself with indecision. And that, Doll, is dangerous."

She looked like she was getting ready to argue some more but before she could open her mouth to utter anymore bullshit, I beat her to it. "And you're wrong. I've been by your side three times now when shit hit the fan. And three times you impressed the hell outta me. I trust your instincts and your judgement. So you can stand here and tell me all about how you don't trust yourself, because at the end of the day, I know it's a lie you're trying to convince yourself of. This is second-nature to you. When we were being chased, you didn't think. Your training took over and you went with your gut. I'd have you at my back, anytime."

"I'm still not sure," she mumbled.

"I'm sure enough for the both of us. Nazari will not be an issue for us. And after tomorrow, he'll no longer be an issue for anyone."

"Okay."

"Are you staying?"

"Yes."

Relief washed over me and I wasn't sure that was such a good thing. I was far more invested in her than I should've been. I was already in too deep, and as the saying went: in for a penny in for a pound. I wasn't pulling back now.

"Great. Go grab your shit. We gotta hit the road."

CHAPTER 21

An hour was a long time to be sitting in an SUV with five irritated men. Well, maybe only four were still annoyed with me. Brooks seemed to have forgiven me for my wishy-washy behavior but, Declan, Max, Kyle, and Thad were all still standoffish. Al Qatif may've only been a forty-five-minute drive according to the map, but traffic at the border crossing was a nightmare. We still had at least another half hour before we arrived and I couldn't take another second of the silence.

"All right, enough. I know why you all are pissed at me, but I can't take it anymore," I blurted out. "Will someone please just tell me I was acting like a whiney bitch so we can get on with it?"

"You're acting like a whiney bitch," Thad said.

Okay, maybe that stung more than I thought it would.

"You ready to spit out whatever the hell is bothering you?" Kyle asked.

No. I wasn't ready. I didn't want to talk about it, but I

was the one who opened the door. Maybe silence wasn't such a bad thing after all.

"Didn't think so," he went on after a beat.

"I fucked up the last time I was in Saudi Arabia. I was stupid and rushed and almost died because of my poor decision making. I don't want anyone else to get hurt because of my stupidity."

"You can't be talking about when you were a POW." Max turned around from the passenger seat to look at me.

"You mean when I got captured because I didn't listen to all my intel? Yeah, Max, that time."

"You can't let that fuck with your head," Thad advised.

"Kinda hard not to when every time I look in the mirror I'm reminded of what an idiot I was."

"Get over it," Declan demanded.

He was driving so he couldn't see the daggers my glare was shooting in his direction and unfortunately, I didn't have any Jedi mind tricks perfected. The ones that would make him go up in a plume of smoke.

"Come again?"

"Didn't stutter, Tatiana."

"No. You didn't, but it was kinda a dick thing to say."

"Seriously? You think you're the first person to be held against their will and take a few hits?"

Was it possible for someone's head to spontaneously combust? Because I think mine was going to explode.

"No, you jackass. I know I'm not. All I'm saying is—"

"That you feel sorry for yourself?"

"Watch it, bro…" Brooks' tone held a whole new meaning of menacing.

I didn't need him to stick up for me, and the last thing

I needed was for the two of them to get into a fight because of me. This was ridiculous.

"I don't feel sorry for myself. I was just explaining why I no longer trust myself."

"Which brings me back to my previous advice. Get over it."

"Okay, Declan. Whatever."

I was stupid for even starting the conversation. I should've known better. All alpha men were the same. Bury it. Lock it down. Don't think about it. Worry about unpacking the cargo container of feelings later when it's busting at the seams ready to spew all over the place.

Real healthy.

"Do you trust me to lead this mission?" Declan asked.

"Yes." If I hadn't been in a car full of men, I would've ignored him.

"Do you trust me to have your back?"

I felt like I was walking into a trap. But I answered anyway, "Yes."

"By your logic, you shouldn't. And I should no longer trust myself. You made a bad play and as a result some assholes took you and *almost* killed you. I fucked up, listened to the wrong person, and got a ten-man platoon captured. Two were murdered before we'd even made it back to the warlord's compound."

Shit, fuck, and damn. I knew this story. I was still with the CIA when it happened. The whole situation down in Panama was a clusterfuck. Declan had sent a Ranger platoon in to take out a high-value target but it was a set-up. His intel was bad and the Rangers were ambushed. From the story I'd heard, Declan had called it in to the higher-ups but didn't wait for backup. He went in alone and saved the remaining eight men. It was a bloody massacre by the time Declan had saved them. The legend went, Dec had single-handedly killed fifteen men. I wasn't privy to the after-action report, however, I believed the rumors. Eight men did indeed come home alive and Declan had no support during the rescue mission.

"That was different," I tried.

"The hell it was. We make do with the information we have in the field. We go on gut feelings. Sometimes it pans out, other times it doesn't. You have to get over it. If you can't, you're gonna be working a desk. Sometimes all you have is a split second and instinct. What happened to you was jacked. But guess what? There's not a man in this vehicle who doesn't bear the scars of battle. Wear that shit proud. You survived."

That was easy for him to say, he wasn't a woman. As sexist as it was, a man bearing the marks of war was acceptable. It made him look tough and manly. Scars on a woman made her undesirable. And when a man fucked up it could be chalked up to a bad day. When a woman did, she was incompetent.

"Not sure our situations were the same."

"You don't think I wasn't where you are? You think I didn't second-guess myself, almost get more people hurt because I was behaving like a pussy who couldn't make up his mind? You think I didn't lie awake at night going over every detail, all the ways I'd screwed up? I beat myself up about it more than anyone else could. Two men went home in a pine box because of me. Two. That's what I live with. I don't need marks on my body to remind me. Their deaths are seared into my skin, on my soul. So what? You fucked up, Tatiana. You rushed your op. Learn from it. Reflect on it. Move on from it. That simple."

It wasn't as simple as Declan made it sound, but he wasn't wrong. If I didn't learn to trust myself again, I'd make more mistakes. Possibly get someone killed. Wasn't that why I was vacillating to begin with? That and the fact I'd never worked with a real team. I hadn't forgotten Zane's warning to me either, these men would give their lives for me, and each other. I needed to sort my shit out, which again, was easier said than done.

"I'm straight," I told him.

"Are you?"

"Yes."

"Great. You and Brooks will go scout Nazari's location when we get to Al Qatif. Max, Thad, you'll take the known locations and restaurants he frequents. Garrett sent over a list. Kyle, you'll stay with me and go over the house blueprints. After a little recon we'll decide the best course of action."

Four men muttered, 'copy that,' and I remained silent thinking about what both Brooks and Declan had told me. Intellectually I knew they were right. But after everything my douchebag ex-husband had drilled into my head, it was hard. Every chance he got he pointed out my inadequacies. Nothing I did was good enough. One time he'd even gone as far as telling me it was a good thing I'd quit the CIA, that I was too weak to be an agent. He'd gone on to say, men were much better suited for field work.

James wasn't always a dick. When I fell in love with him, he was kind and supportive. He'd valued my opinions and often praised my insight on situations and subjects. But after we got married he changed. And when he got pulled from deployment rotation and was sent to X Division at the SEAL training command, he really changed. He turned into a mean asshole and always had something to complain about.

It was hard to trust yourself after you'd been really wrong about two life-changing situations. Bottom line was, I had to pull my shit together or Declan was right, I was better off behind a desk.

Brooks reached over and picked up my hand, interlacing our fingers. He gave it a squeeze before resting our hands back on the seat between us. I closed my eyes and soaked up all the support and encouragement Brooks was offering. I hadn't known how much I needed it.

Please God, don't let Brooks be my third big mistake.

CHAPTER 22

"You ever clean your binos?" Tatiana asked, pulling the night vision binoculars away from her face. "There're smudge marks on the lenses."

She wasn't wrong. Whoever had used them last, had put them away dirty.

We'd dropped off the team at the house we were spending the night in and headed to recon Nazari's location. I was happy to see Tatiana seemed to have snapped out of her funk. Declan as usual hadn't pulled punches while we were in the car and gave it to her straight. On the best of days, he could come across as harsh if you didn't know him. He didn't massage the truth to make it sound pretty. He could and did bullshit with all of us, but when it was time to get serious, he cut right to it. One of the many things I liked about him. He also held his cards close to his vest and showed little emotion. I could appreciate the need for the mask he wore – he may've been full of bravado while he was speaking to Tatiana, but I knew that shit that happened in Panama marked him deep. He wasn't over it, and the more he gave Tatiana advice the more it sounded like he was trying to give himself a mental pep talk.

"Any sign of Nazari?" I asked, ignoring her comment.

"No. Just his two sons are visible," she said, lifting the NVGs back to her eyes. "Maybe he's out somewhere with his daughter. We haven't seen her yet, either. Or he could already be asleep."

"Either is possible." I checked my watch and it was nearing ten p.m. "How old is the daughter again?"

"Twenty-three."

"And she's not married?"

"Weird, right? Normally a woman her age would've been married off."

It was unusual, especially coming from a respected family.

"I didn't read anything about his wife, where is she?"

The more I thought about it, the more I realized I needed to comb over the files Garrett had sent over on Nazari and his family.

"Dead. Lots of rumors about cause of death but nothing has ever been confirmed. Someone's pulling in the gate."

I shifted my focus from the back area of the house to the front driveway. A light-colored sedan rolled to a stop and Nazari stepped out of the driver's side door, walked around the hood, and opened the passenger door. A tall, slender woman stepped out of the car. Even through the green tint of my NVGs I could see how dark her long hair was.

"That's his daughter, Sefa."

I watched as Nazari pulled her close and nuzzled Sefa's neck. He took his time, and if I wasn't mistaken, he'd kissed the skin below her ear.

"Ew. That's gross." I could picture Tatiana scrunching her cute nose as she spoke.

Nazari's head lifted and the woman smiled brightly before she leaned forward and kissed him on the mouth.

"I think someone needs to double-check Sefa Nazari's birth certificate. I'm not sure I've ever seen a daughter kiss her father that way. And if she is his kid, I never want to see that shit again," I grouched.

Just when I thought the scene before us couldn't get any worse, Nazari deepened the kiss and grabbed the woman's ass. I hoped to God, someone, somewhere got their wires crossed and their intel wrong because this shit was whacked. He was full on making out with the woman. There was so much wrong with what we were witnessing. First, if he was her dad, he had serious fucking mental issues. The age gap couldn't be denied, he *looked* old enough to be her father. He was fifty-nine and looked every bit his years and then some. He was the same height as the woman but where she was thin, he was rounded.

"I can't watch this shit," Tatiana complained. "It's disgusting."

"There's no way she's his daughter. Are you sure that's Sefa?"

"One-hundred percent. I've tailed her, sat a table over while she had lunch with her friends in Bahrain. I've also seen surveillance footage of her and Nazari together. Not like this. The images I saw, they looked very much like father and daughter."

The couple broke apart and Nazari led her toward the house, still holding her hand. They disappeared out of sight for a moment before we picked them back up through the large windows in the back of the house. We had a clear view of the room the sons were sitting in. When Nazari and Sefa entered the room hand in hand, both of the sons looked in their direction but otherwise didn't move. A few minutes later, Sefa's hand grazed Nazari's face before she kissed him again square on the mouth. Neither son seemed to care that their *sister* was extra friendly with daddy.

"I feel like I'm watching a really bad porn movie," she muttered.

"Yeah? You watch daddy kink porn often?"

"No!" she huffed.

"Right. So just regular porn then. Got it."

"I don't watch any porn."

"So, how would you know this is bad porn?"

"I'm not even going to answer that. You know what I meant."

Sefa exited the room, leaving the three men alone. Nazari sat in a chair across from the couch his sons were lounging on and calmly engaged in conversation. A minute later a light turned on upstairs, illuminating a bedroom. From our vantage point we could clearly make out the door leading to the hall, a bed, and bureau. I lost sight of Sefa when she walked to the far end of the room.

"No, I'm not sure what you meant. I think I need to hear more about what type of porn you enjoy."

"We're not having this discussion," she told me.

Sefa come back into view. She'd changed into a long nightgown. If I had to guess I'd say it was satin. She stood next to the bed brushing her hair, smiling to herself. She looked happy. Not like I would expect a daughter to look if her father was forcing her into some kind of sick relationship.

"It looks like they're going to sleep." I glanced back into the living area where the men had been sitting. They were now up, turning off lights, and all three were heading toward the stairs. "I don't think I want to see what happens next."

Neither did I. If it turned out Nazari was indeed Sefa's father, the kiss we'd witnessed was all I could take. The older of the two sons stepped into the doorway and Sefa turned but stayed in place. The man walked into the room, shut the door behind him, and did not waste any time moving to her side. His mouth was on hers and he was pulling her nightgown up. Not to be outdone, Sefa pawed at his shirt and got it over his head.

"I've seen enough."

I had to agree. So had I. I moved my binoculars away from the window as the man was yanking the nightgown over Sefa's head.

"This is some fucked-up shit."

"Nazari is in his room," she told me.

"Son number two is in his," I returned.

"Great. Mission complete. Hurry up, I need a shower after seeing that. Maybe find some sort of voodoo pill to erase the last ten minutes of my life."

I stood and held out my hand to Tatiana. I was fully

prepared for her to bitch about me wanting to help her up. Imagine my surprise when she simply took it and allowed me to pull her to her feet.

"Thanks," she murmured.

"Come on, I think I have just the thing that will help you forget what you just saw," I told her, as we made our way down the small embankment leading to the side of Nazari's house. I noted several points of entry. His security was weak. He didn't even have a bodyguard with him.

"I don't think that's possible."

"Doll, by the time I'm done with you, you won't be thinking about anything other than how amazing you feel."

"Cocky much?"

"Just laying it out for you."

"Did you miss the part where I said I wanted a shower?"

"Yeah, I heard you. And as I remember, the shower was pretty fucking good. Though I prefer you in a bed where I can—"

"You can stop now."

We'd made it back to the car and I opened the passenger door for her but stopped her before she could get in.

"Just think about all the delicious things I'm gonna do to your body when we get home."

Tatiana rocked back and her eyes came to mine. Even in the dark I could see desire swirling. Damn she was sexy.

CHAPTER 23

"She did what?" Declan asked.

We'd just finished telling the guys about the make-out session we'd witnessed.

"Oh, no, it gets worse," I told him. "After that, Sefa went upstairs. Her older brother, Kadar, followed. I stopped watching when the two of them started going at it."

"Last thing I saw was Kadar removing her nightgown," Brooks added.

"What the fuck?" Thad's eyes were wide in horror. "There's no way she's related to them."

"For argument's sake, let's say she's not the daughter. Then who is she? And is she there of her own free will? And is there a real daughter?"

"Don't know. But she was smiling and it didn't look like she was disgusted or being forced. When Kadar and her started going at it, she was trying to get his clothes off," I told him.

"So what? She's some sort of mistress they share? Did the younger one..."

"Tahir," I provided.

"Did Tahir get any action?" Kyle finished.

"Nope. Just dear ole dad and big brother," Brooks answered.

"That's fucked. Don't even joke about it." Max shook his head.

"I'll call this in to Garrett and Tex. Hopefully they can get to the bottom of this." Declan's gaze landed on mine and he asked, "Seriously, full on make-out session?"

"Yes. Ass grabbing included. Right in front of the house."

The whole scene was forever imprinted on my mind. I really hoped the intel was bad and Sefa was not Matek Nazari's daughter. It wasn't like it would be all that hard for a man like Nazari to get a forged birth certificate made. If that was the case, the question was, why the hell go through all the trouble? It wasn't like it would've been frowned upon for him to take a new wife after the first one died. The age difference wouldn't even be an issue. The whole situation was bizarre. And totally gross.

"I don't feel comfortable engaging on an unknown woman," Declan said. "If she's an innocent being forced into some sort of sex... I don't even know what to call what they're doing. Bottom line is, we're not going in until we have good intel on the woman."

Everyone gave their agreeance but something was bothering me.

"I don't think she's a victim," I told the guys.

"Why?" Kyle asked.

"I've followed her. She goes out alone, meets with friends. There are no guards. If she's being held against her will, there have been plenty of times she could've escaped."

"There are many ways to force someone into a situation. You don't always need guns and guards to do it," Declan reminded me.

"There are, yes. But she's complicit in his smuggling operation. I've seen it. My gut is telling me she's an opportunist, not a victim."

I regretted my words as soon as I'd said them. Why would anyone in the room take me seriously after our discussion in the car? I'd admitted I didn't trust myself anymore, yet there I was telling the team I only had a gut feeling, no facts to go on.

"You could be right. Let's see what Tex and Garrett dig up and we'll go from there."

That was Declan's way of nicely dismissing my opinion. I appreciated he hadn't called me out in front of everyone.

"And for the record, Tatiana, if you believe she's in on it, I trust your insight. I'm not questioning you. I just think we need to know more about this woman and where she came from."

"What did you guys find?" Brooks asked Max and Thad.

"Nothing useful," Thad answered. "Just confirmation he's been seen in the area."

"I'm gonna grab a beer. Anyone else?" Kyle asked, already walking toward the kitchen.

"A beer?" I questioned.

"One of the many perks of working for Z Corps. Fully stocked fridge in all our safehouses," Brooks informed me.

The other four men called out their yeses. As good as a beer sounded, a shower sounded even better.

"I'm gonna get a shower in first," I told the guys.

Brooks' gaze shifted to mine and a wicked smile tugged at his lips. Tingles hit me in all the right places and with great difficulty I kept my face blank. Visions of his naughty promise filled my mind, I had to get away from him before I lost the battle and my cheeks heated.

Not waiting for anyone to acknowledge my announcement, I left the room as quickly as I could without looking like I was fleeing a crime scene. By the masculine chuckles behind me, I'd failed. Whatever. I was beyond being embarrassed. Not to mention, the condo we were now staying in only had three bedrooms. Two of the rooms had two twin-sized beds and the third had only one bed. A full-sized. *Guess which room I was assigned to?* A full-sized bed was barely big enough for a man Brooks' size. The two of us would be crammed on top of each other. The thought made the tingling from earlier reappear. In an effort to not think about tonight's sleeping arrangements, I opened my backpack and rummaged through the contents, finding something clean to change into.

My cell phone vibrated, startling me. Shit, I'd forgotten I hadn't checked in with Leon in over twelve hours. Was I still supposed to be checking in with him? Z Corps had officially taken over my employment and neither Zane nor Leon had clarified who I was working for. Just because Zane was now signing my paychecks didn't mean I no longer worked for The Company.

I found my phone as the call went to voicemail. Three missed calls from Leon. Interesting. He'd never called three times back to back before. Not bothering to check the voicemails he's left, I returned his call.

"There you are," he barked.

"Hello, Leon. How are you?"

My question was met with silence. He was probably rolling his eyes at my attempt of politeness.

"Great. Listen, there's been a shift. I have a job for you."

"Okay." I drew the word out and unease hit my stomach.

"Sefa Nazari."

"What about her?"

"She's your target."

"My target? Our orders are Nazari and only his children if they engage."

"That may be the orders Zane has given *his* men. However, your objective is Sefa Nazari. You have two hours. I'll expect an update when the job is done. And one more thing. This is need to know and none of the men you are with need to know."

The unease I'd felt moments ago turned into apprehension. I was no stranger to top secret directives. The assassination order didn't even bother me. It wasn't the first and it wouldn't be the last. What I didn't like was having to keep secrets from the team.

"Did you hear me?"

"I heard you."

"You have two hours."

"Copy that."

Leon disconnected and I tossed my phone on the bed. I couldn't forget what Zane had told me about Z Corps being a better option than The Company. And I still wasn't sure what he meant when he told me he knew more about them than I did, but less than he should. I worked with Leon for years, he'd never given me any indication I couldn't trust him, so why was I second-guessing his orders now? I shouldn't have been questioning anything. I had a direct order, one that I needed to obey.

"Everything okay?"

"Jesus." I startled and turned toward the doorway with my heart damn near in my throat. "Yeah. Everything's fine."

"You sure? You look like you're weighing something big over there."

"Nope. Just thinking about Sefa and Nazari," I semi-lied.

I *was* thinking about Sefa, just not the way I'd allowed Brooks believe I was. I'd already started to plan how I'd take her out. I only had two hours. That was not a lot of time to shower, sneak away from the team, complete my mission, and come back.

"Yeah, that shit was pretty jacked," he returned.

I picked up my clean clothes, phone, and started for the door.

"It was. Time to wash the ick off." I shouldered past him, ignoring the 'what the fuck' look he gave me and made my way down the hallway to the one bathroom we'd all have to share. I quickly shut the door and tuned the lock before Brooks followed me in and started asking questions.

No sooner had I turned the taps on, undressed, and stepped under the shower spray, guilt hit me hard. I'd lied to Brooks. Not the way I had to keep my cover when we'd first met, but straight out. And in ten minutes I was going to lie to the rest of the team and sneak away. Leon would text me the location where I could pick up a weapon and I would assassinate a woman we'd all agreed to gather more intel on. My conscience wouldn't shut up and neither would Zane's nagging voice, reminding me these men would take a bullet for me.

Fuck.

My hair was barely wet when I jerked the spigot handle and turned the water off. I yanked a towel off the hook and angrily dried my body. I couldn't do it. Taking out Sefa wasn't the issue. Lying, turning my back on the team, was. And it wouldn't be one lie. They'd all pile on top of each other. Sneaking away was just the tip of the iceberg. Tomorrow when they found out she was dead, more lies would follow. When they investigated who took her out, even more lies would mount.

Then there was the other problem I had. Zane. I'd never known him to be a bullshitter. He had the best instincts in the business and he'd admitted, not in so many words, there was something about The Company he didn't like. He wouldn't have told me working for him was a better option if he hadn't had misgivings about the people I worked for. I didn't know if it was Leon Brown he didn't trust or The Company as a whole. Either was a good enough reason to give me pause.

With clean clothes on, I went in search of the guys. I found them all except Brooks, sitting around the dining room table.

"Where's Brooks?" I asked.

Four sets of eyes swung my way. All of them with matching looks of curiosity.

"Right here," he said from behind me and walked into the dining area.

With a deep inhale, I prayed I was doing the right thing. Not only was I breaking protocol, I was getting ready to break operational security. I glanced down at the phone in my hand and thought better about speaking freely with the device in the room.

I held up the phone with one hand and gestured with the other to give me a minute. After running back to the bedroom, shoving the phone into my backpack and shutting the door, I felt better about going against Leon's order not to tell the team.

"What's wrong?" Declan asked as soon as I reentered the room.

"When I went back to the room, I had three missed calls from my handler. When I returned the call, he informed me I had a new assignment."

"What? He's pulling you?" Brooks asked.

"No. He gave me a two hour clock to assassinate Sefa Nazari."

"What the fuck?" Declan stood. "Zane didn't say anything about that."

"He doesn't know about the mission shift. My orders are need to know. I was specifically told none of you were to be in the know."

Well, I now knew how to get a room full of operatives stunned into silence. The men all exchanged looks and waited for someone to say something. Declan's face turned to stone, and Brooks looked like he was getting ready to explode.

Great.

CHAPTER 24

Long moments ticked by before Tatiana spoke, "Anyone?"

I suppose she was waiting for someone to say something, but it wasn't going to be me. I was too fucking pissed to utter a word.

"Let me see if I understand," Declan started. "Leon agreed to lend you to Z Corps for the mission. Then he calls you and gives you a side job to take out Sefa, but wants it kept from the team. I get that right?"

"Yes."

"There's no interpretation? Straight out he said you were not to tell us?" he asked again.

Tatiana's eyes rolled and she answered, "Yes, Declan. His words were, it was need to know and none of you needed to know. He gave me two hours to complete my assignment."

"Then why are you breaking security protocol?" I asked.

"Huh?" Her eyes moved from Dec to me and they looked wounded that I'd questioned her.

"You were specifically ordered not to tell us, yet here you are passing on information on a mission you were given. One I assume, would be classified as top secret. Your ass should be out the door carrying out your task."

Tatiana squared her shoulders and the woman who I'd met the first day in Bahrain was back. Expressionless. Assessing. Cold.

"The order from my team leader was hold fast and wait for new intel. Not only that but we'd all agreed more information was needed on Sefa before we moved. Zane has not weighed in and given further instructions. Until that time, I'm following Declan's direction."

"Leon Brown is your handler. Not Zane. Not Declan. So, again, why the hell are you standing here and not following orders?" I pushed.

I needed more. More than Leon Brown and Zane Lewis having what I believe was a pissing contest with Tatiana stuck in the middle.

"Declan said—"

"Bullshit. You work for The Company, not Z Corps."

"I work for Z Corps on this mission," she argued.

"Again. I call bullshit. What you've done is akin to subversion. Best case, you'll be terminated. Most likely they send someone after you to eliminate what they'll feel is a loose end."

Tatiana's face lost the mask of indifference and she leaned forward, unleashing her fury. "It feels like a lie," she said through gritted teeth. "Something is not right. Sefa Nazari has never been on radar for a hit. Why now? Why her and not Matek? He's always been the one we've watched. Now after tonight and what we saw, why is Sefa suddenly on The Company's list?"

"What feels like a lie?" Declan asked, beating me to it.

"Sneaking away and killing a woman we all agreed we needed more intel on. Leaving and not telling anyone. Leon telling me that *my* team doesn't need to know. All of it. It's all wrong."

That was what I needed to know. Where her loyalty was. Even though her telling us about Leon's assignment should've told me, it didn't. Her explaining she didn't want to be dishonest was what I needed to hear to continue to trust her.

"How are you supposed to carry out the kill?" Kyle asked.

Apparently, he, too, had gotten the answers he needed.

"My discretion."

"And weapons?" Thad inquired.

"I should be getting a text any minute if I haven't already with a nearby location where someone will supply me with what I need."

"Did he tell you that?" Declan questioned.

"No. Standard operating procedure. I can't have a weapons cache when I'm supposed to be working for the UN or relief organizations. There's always someone who provides me with anything I need."

"Does this happen often, getting a kill order in the middle of a mission?" Dec continued.

"Not often. But it's happened a few times."

I had to admit I didn't like the mission shift with an order to kill a woman we'd just finished surveilling. The calls to Tatiana started before Declan had called in what we saw to Zane. So how would Leon Brown, who was presumably in the United States, know we'd had Sefa in our sights earlier in the night?

I looked around at my team and they, too, were all trying to puzzle out why the kill order had come in at that moment in time if there had never been any mention of her being a target before. Maybe it was something as innocent as Leon finding new intel on the woman and deeming her a high threat. But that didn't explain why he wanted Tatiana to go in alone.

"Are there any issues between Leon Brown and Zane?" I asked Declan.

"Not that Z said."

"Zane told me working for him was a better option than working for The Company," Tatiana added. "But he didn't elaborate. He also said he didn't have as much intel on them as he'd like."

Declan pulled out his cell and dialed, putting it on speaker. It took four rings before Zane answered, "Yeah."

"Is there an issue between you and Leon Brown we should know about?"

Zane's laughter filled the room. "Wouldn't surprise me. I've pissed off a lot of people. Why?"

"He sent Tatiana on a mission. Need to know, with us in the dark."

"What kind of mission?" Zane's tone had changed from humorous to deadly.

Tatiana spoke up, filling Zane in on what Leon had told her. Once she was done, he remained quiet for a moment. When he finally spoke again you could feel his anger rolling off in waves, over the phone, and thousands of miles away, it didn't matter. When Zane Lewis was pissed the world knew it.

"The Company is a division of the CIA. Their latest and greatest attempt at complete anonymity. When I say complete, I mean, complete. Off the books and black ops. No records are kept. None. Only verbal communication between the handlers and their operatives. Handlers verbally report in to one man. No paper trail whatsoever."

"If there's no electronic footprint, how'd you find it?" Thad asked.

"I have my sources. Take the mission. If Leon is keeping tabs, he needs to think you'll still follow his orders. I need a few hours to figure out what game Leon is playing."

"Take the mission?" Tatiana questioned. "We don't have all the intel. We were going to wait."

"Brooks, take her back. You're a shadow. I don't want you seen unless shit goes sideways. This could also be a trap. Get Tatiana separated from the team so he can take her out. Be ready for anything. I don't trust a goddamn thing the CIA does."

"I want to be clear, Zane," Tatiana said. "Are you telling me to execute the order?"

"No. I want you to accept the mission. Pick up your weapon. Go to the location and wait. Garrett is almost done. What he's finding doesn't look good for Sefa Nazari, however it doesn't amount to a death sentence. Unless Tex comes up with something more, you'll report back to Leon and explain why you failed."

"But I've never failed," Tatiana complained.

She was cute when she grumbled about having to report an unsuccessful mission.

"I think your stats will survive," Zane joked. "Twenty-and-oh is nothing to sneeze at."

"Twenty confirmed?" Kyle asked, his voice laced with respect.

With a nod she verified his question. Nothing about her posture indicated she was proud of the number of assassinations she'd carried out or the fact that she'd executed his orders without fail. Another bit of information slid into place and I was beginning to understand her a little more.

"Goddamn. Thought you said this type of thing doesn't happen often," Kyle continued.

"Define often." She wasn't asking him a question, simply offering an answer. "Okay, so I fail the take down. What then? Call him back and tell him I couldn't get to her?"

"Yes. Unless Tex or Garrett finds something. But so far, I'm not seeing anything."

"Fine," she huffed.

"Declan, if this is a trap you need to be ready for anything. Maybe this has to do with us. He could want her out of the house so he can take out the team and save her. Be ready for anything. Trust no one outside of you six."

I was happy to see Zane had included Tatiana in the circle of trust.

"One more thing. Good work, Tatiana." Zane, always the one to get in the last word, hung up.

Declan immediately started putting together a plan. He, Kyle, Thad, and Max would stay behind. He and Max would take patrol around the block and Thad and Kyle would take watch inside the condo. I'd be shadowing Tatiana. I hated not having a clear understanding of any given scenario, but I really fucking hated walking into a trap.

"You ready? Time's ticking," I told Tatiana after Declan was done.

"Yeah. Let me grab my phone."

Max had been suspiciously quiet throughout the entire conversation, but when Tatiana left the room, he spoke.

"Watch your back."

"Always do," I answered, as I finished strapping my tac vest on.

"No. I mean, watch your back. Z was polite enough not to run through one more option in front of Tatiana, but there's a chance—"

"I got it," I snapped, unwilling to listen to Max tell me there was a possibility Tatiana was in on whatever play Leon was making.

"All right," Max muttered and walked away.

His acquiesces couldn't have happened at a better time. Tatiana entered the room kitted out in her gear. I looked her over and still had a hard time reconciling the dichotomy. Soft, beautiful, sexy female to the cold, tough, assassin with twenty verified kills and zero misses. Yeah, that was something I would've never guessed.

CHAPTER 25

"You okay?" Brooks asked after we'd been driving for about ten minutes.

"Peachy."

"You don't sound peachy."

That was because I wasn't. But I didn't want to talk to Brooks about my stupid life choices. How could I have been so fucking dumb taking a job I knew nothing about? After Zane had said there was no paper trail, which in this day and age meant electronic transmissions, it hit me I'd never received any mission briefs via email or text. I'd scrolled through my phone to confirm what I already knew. I had text messages with addresses but no instructions. I had emails with new job listings and HR contacts but nothing that wouldn't look like a recruiter trying to help me get a new job. I had emails asking how I was doing, updates on my whereabouts, but those looked like they'd come from a concerned friend, not my fucking CIA handler.

The worst part, I'd known. Deep in my gut I knew The Company had ties to the CIA. How could they not? I was running the same types of operations. The only thing that had changed were the rules of engagement. Or should I say the lack thereof. Leon had given me orders and I'd followed them to the letter. Zane was right, I was rogue. The CIA had practically invented the meaning of disavow. But this was a whole new level. They wouldn't have to deny I was working a job if it went sideways and I was caught somewhere I shouldn't have been. Because I legitimately no longer worked for the government. I was a goddamned contract killer, minus the outrageous pay they received for their kills. In my mind, there was a huge difference carrying out assignments my government deemed valuable, and this. This was shit. However, I had no one to blame but myself. Maybe James was right, I was too stupid to work for the CIA.

Dammit to hell. Fuck Leon Brown. Screw The Company. I was the dumbest woman on the planet.

"Well, I am peachy," I told Brooks. "The house is a few blocks up. Park anywhere. I'll walk the rest of the way."

"Not gonna happen."

"What part of shadow did you not understand? You can't park out front. Someone will see you," I reminded him.

Brooks drove a little way more and pulled over. Before I could get out of the car, he grabbed my bicep and stopped me. "Watch your back."

His words stung. They were the same ones Max had told him when I'd left the room and he thought I couldn't hear. Max didn't trust me and Brooks hadn't said anything. Not that I actually blamed him. I had contemplated carrying out my assignment without telling them. But I wasn't in on whatever Leon was planning. That was the part that hurt. Max had thought I would hurt one of them. Forgetting everything that had happened between me and Brooks privately, I'd never betray him, or any of them. Not like that. And the fact that Max thought I was capable of it bothered me.

"I got it." I tried to yank my arm away but Brooks held fast.

"I'm serious, Doll. We don't know what Leon's playing at. This could be an ambush. If something doesn't feel right, it's not. Shoot first, and we'll sort it out later."

Brooks' look of concern gave me pause. And that irked me, too. "What about you? Are you watching your six?"

I don't know why I asked him that. I wasn't going to bring up what I'd overheard but the words slipped out.

"That's your job. We're partners, remember?"

"And if it's me who's been sent to sink the knife in your back?"

"Not concerned. I trust you." I hadn't realized how much I needed to hear him say that. "Don't worry about Max. He has trust issues."

I was happy he hadn't played dumb and pretended not to know what I was referring to. It didn't help knowing Max didn't trust easily. The bottom line remained, it was me he didn't have faith in.

"I'll be careful," I told him, getting back to the original topic of conversation.

Brooks wordlessly let go of me and I exited the car. I had less than a block to walk before the house came into view. It was dark and there were plenty of places for someone to hide. Unease crept in and I just wanted to hurry and pick up whatever Leon had sent me to retrieve.

When I approached the house, an older man was waiting outside. He immediately handed me a black rifle case.

"Everything is there," he told me.

"Thanks."

I slowly turned my back on the man and hoped like hell he wasn't planning on shooting me as I walked away. Though I knew Brooks was out there somewhere, I couldn't see him, but I could feel him. The thought made me smile. There was no way Brooks would let me walk into an unknown situation and not have his scope trained on the man I was meeting.

Maybe it should've annoyed me. I'd been going at this alone for a long time. I was more than capable of handling myself. Though I didn't have eyes in the back of my head and wouldn't know if I was getting ready to take two to the skull.

That was a lovely thought. Great job I had. Most people went to work and the only thing they had to worry about was a paper cut or maybe at worst a slip and fall. Me? Bullets, blood, and mayhem were only the tip of my worries.

I slipped into the back seat of the car at the same time as Brooks got behind the wheel. Just as I'd thought, he followed me.

"See anything?" I asked, unzipping the soft, padded rifle case.

"He had a spotter. Top-floor window."

"He's an arms' dealer. I suppose that is normal," I reminded him. "Hey, you got a pen light up there?"

Brooks handed me back a small LED flashlight. I clicked it on and inspected the contents of the case.

"What'd they give you?" Brooks asked.

"A .338 Lapua. Ziess optics," I told him.

"Sweet rig."

He wasn't wrong. The .338 bolt action was a pretty rifle, my favorite as a matter of fact. Though if I had my choice, I would've switched out the optics for a Night-Force scope. Beggars can't be choosers and I wasn't the one who'd purchased the set-up. Which got me thinking.

"Who do you think funds The Company?" I asked Brooks, as I continued to inspect the rifle.

"My guess would be it comes out of the congressional fund, earmarked for something else. You know the bull-shit games our government plays with our tax dollars."

"What the fuck?" I muttered, shining the flashlight down the bolt carrier group of the rifle.

"What?"

"There's no fucking firing pin," I told him.

"Come again?"

"Those motherfuckers. They removed the firing pin."

Son of a bitch. You can't shoot a weapon with no firing pin. And it doesn't just fall out on its own. Someone would've had to purposefully disassemble the bolt carrier group, unscrew the firing pin assembly, and taken the long pin out. It wasn't like you wouldn't notice a four-inch piece of metal that looked like a paperclip unfolded and straightened out lying around when you reassembled the weapon.

"Don't suppose you have a gunsmith kit with extra parts lying around, do you?" I tried to joke off my supreme anger.

Leon Brown was sending me into a trap. Who was meant to get caught remained to be seen.

"Brooks?" I called when he didn't answer.

"What?"

"Never mind."

All righty then. Someone was pissed off. I wasn't sure why he was so mad, it was me that Leon had potentially gotten killed. You only sabotaged someone's weapon when you didn't want them to be able to shoot back when you came shooting at them.

"Sorry. I'm thinking."

"About what?"

"Trying to figure out if there's a way I can convince you to keep your ass in the car when we get to Nazari's."

"Not a chance."

With a heavy sigh he answered, "Didn't think so."

I put the useless rifle back into the case, placed it on the back seat, and climbed over the center console and settled into the passenger seat.

"You think he sent someone to take me out?" I asked.

"Yes."

"I have to admit this is getting old."

"What is?"

"People trying to kill me. And now, Leon. What. The. Fuck."

We were approaching Nazari's house. I didn't have time to think about all the new information that had come to light in the last hour, especially the fact that the US government now wanted me dead, too.

"When we get out, you stay at my back," Brooks told me as he found a place to park.

"No way. Nothing's changed. I'll take the back, you walk the perimeter. It will be faster."

"Everything has changed," he argued.

Brooks pulled his phone out of his cargos, cutting off any further rebuttal.

"Yeah." There was a pause, then his eyes widened and he replied, "No shit." Another pause. "Never had to worry about Tatiana taking a shot, anyway. Brown gave her nonop. The firing pin was removed. We're going to walk the perimeter and we'll be back." He looked over at me and said, "Copy that."

"What'd he say?" I asked as soon as Brooks hung up.

"You're never gonna believe this shit. Sefa Nazari is CIA. Her name is Ashaki Maloof. American born. Her parents are both naturalized US citizens."

"I'm not seeing Leon's play. Is she supposed to kill me? And why the hell did Nazari go through the trouble of making people believe she is his daughter?"

"Hell if I know. Declan wants one look around and for us to get our asses back to the condo."

"Sounds good. I'll take the left and meet you around the back."

"Fine."

"Are you pouting?" I laughed.

Even in the dim moonlight, I couldn't deny how good-looking he was. I had to admit, I was a little disappointed that his promise of helping me forget seeing Sefa – or

Ashaki as it were – making out with whom I thought were her father and brother, had been interrupted.

"Men don't pout, Doll."

"It sure looks like you are."

"Why don't you just announce to the entire neighborhood we're here?"

I pinched my lips together in an effort not to laugh at his obvious attempt to deflect. He was totally pouting because he wasn't getting his way and I wasn't going to stay by his side like he wanted.

He walked a few steps ahead of me and my mind went straight into the gutter. He had a great ass. It was firm, and I remembered how his muscles had flexed under my hands as I held on while he was on top of me thrusting deep. I had to have been the craziest woman alive. There I was, walking down a dark street with the possibility of death looming over my head, and all I could think about was how I hoped I'd get to have more sex with Brooks.

It's good to know I had my priorities in order.

Not.

CHAPTER 26

I watched as Tatiana disappeared into the shadows and wondered if there would ever be a time she'd do as I asked. My step faltered mid-stride as a very uncomfortable question hit me, would there even be a next time? Would she continue to work for Z Corps after this mission or would she... be on her way? Surely she wouldn't go back to working for Leon Brown. The douchebag was up to something.

Who gave the order to have the firing pin removed from her weapon, making it completely inoperable, remained to be seen. Maybe the whole kill order was bogus and he was testing her loyalty to him. It was a plausible scenario; tell her there was a mission shift, it was top secret, and send her out with the intention of actually having her kill Sefa. It was dangerous and stupid but not beyond the realm of possibility for an asshole like him. Or was he trying to get her killed?

All the fine hairs on my neck stood on end and dread coated my gut. Fuck.

Before I could turn, the barrel of a gun was pointed to the back of my head.

"I would've thought the stupid bitch learned her lesson," a thick Middle-Eastern accent spoke from behind me. "The prince doesn't like people—"

The sound of suppressed gunfire took me by surprise. A millisecond after I realized I hadn't been the one hit, I swung toward the sound and saw Tatiana still had her weapon aimed at the dead man on the ground.

I yanked my phone out and took a photo of what was left of the man's face. It was debatable if Garrett or Tex would be able to run a facial recognition trace, but I'd rather I had something to give them. I patted the man down, took his phone, and as I was straightening, I noticed a tattoo.

"Fuck."

"What?"

"He's Omni," I said, pointing at the peacock feather tattoo.

"How do you know?"

Not having the time for a lengthy explanation, I gave her the basics. "We had trouble back in the states. All the men who worked Omni had the same peacock feather tattoo. Let's roll before we have company." I picked up the gun with two fingers, trying to preserve any fingerprints we could pull.

Without a word she followed me back to the car down the street. Even with a silencer on her sidearm, I'm sure we'd woken a Nazari or at least a few of their neighbors.

Contrary to what most people thought, a suppressor did not silence the sound of gunfire. It merely stifled it —barely.

"What the hell was that?" she asked once we'd gotten into the car. "How the hell did he know where we were?"

"Good fucking question. Call Declan, would'ya?"

She pulled her phone out, and after dialing, lifted it to her face. A few seconds ticked by before she ended the call. "No answer."

"Dammit."

I slammed the gas pedal to the floor. We made it back to the area the condo was in half the time it should've taken.

"That van's new," Tatiana said.

"New how?"

"It wasn't there when we left."

"Was that gunfire?" she asked and rolled down the window.

It didn't take long for another volley of shots to ring out.

I slammed on the brakes, the vehicle going from fifty to zero in seconds. We came to a sliding stop and before I could tell her not to move, Tatiana was out of the car running toward the condo.

Christ Almighty, she was going to be the death of me. No plan. No discussion. She just bolted. Not bothering to turn off the car, I jogged in the direction she'd gone. There'd been no gunfire in at least two minutes but that didn't mean jack shit. Luckily, I found Tatiana crouched behind a cement wall, gun drawn, watching.

"I don't see anyone," she whispered.

Hyper-aware of our surroundings, I listened and watched. Not seeing any movement, I pointed forward and she nodded. Fortunately, she let me take the lead. I could feel her close, matching me stride for stride. We slowly approached the condo; no shots fired, no movement.

I heard three sharp whistles and turned to Tatiana. "We're all clear."

"How do you know?"

"We don't always have the luxury of radio communication. Three fast, consecutive whistles is our code," I explained. "Keep your eyes open."

We continued to make our way to the front of the condo. Max turned his gun and pointed directly at Tatiana. In the dim light I could see his face was hard and he was pissed.

"What the fuck?" I muttered. "Lower your weapon."

"You," he spit out.

I glanced over at Tatiana and shockingly she was lowering her gun and holstering it even though Max had not done the same. I wouldn't have blamed her if she'd continued to take aim.

"What. The. Fuck," I repeated.

"You in on this bullshit?" he asked, nodding to his right. My gaze followed where he was gesturing and I saw two men covered in blood crumpled on the ground. Both very dead.

She hadn't taken her eyes off Max. Hadn't moved.

"I suggest you lower your gun." There was no mistaking the anger in her voice.

"*I* suggest we all go inside before we get sniped." I tried to calm the situation.

"And what happens if I don't? You gonna send in another hit squad to try and take us all out?"

Her body jerked back like he'd physically struck her. "Is anyone injured?" she asked, before I could question Max.

"Lucky for you, no. It's the only reason you're still breathin'."

"What the—"

"You think I did this? I sent them?" she cut me off.

Max continued. "Funny thing is, before today I was starting to trust you. But I don't believe in coincidences. Before you showed up, no one was shooting at us. Before you, we had a clear-cut mission. Before you, it was a quick in and out. Now everywhere we go, we're fucked and the only thing that has changed is you."

"Are you fucking crazy?" She stepped toward Max. At that moment in time, I'd say they both were. He was making wild accusations and she was stepping closer to a very pissed off, deadly man pointing a gun at her. "I'm gonna ask you one more time to stop pointing your gun at me. I see you're upset. But I'm unclear how you've drawn the conclusion I want any of you dead."

"Upset? You haven't seen upset, woman."

I'd had enough. I moved between Max and Tatiana and held my friend's stare. "She saved my life tonight. One of Al Issa's men got the drop on me. Pointblank to the back of the head. If Tatiana had been one second later, I'd be dead. Tell me, does that play into whatever fucked-up scenario you have swirling around in your head? If she'd set this whole thing up, why'd she save me?"

Declan walked outside and entered our standoff. "I totally fucking get it now. I always thought Zane just liked being an asshole. Thought he got off on watching everyone scramble when he growled and barked orders. I was wrong. Really wrong. He's an asshole because trying to keep all of you pricks straight is a feat unto itself. I need divine intervention." Dec stopped by Max's side and continued, "Put your fucking gun away. You're not gonna shoot anyone. But I'm afraid Tatiana may kick you in the testicles the next time you're not looking."

"What happened here?" I asked.

"From what I heard you tell Max, it sounds like the same shit that happened to you. Those two over there tried to take a few shots. Other than Dickhead Number One's bullet nearly taking Max's head off, they didn't get close to gaining entry. By the way, you think we can all go inside now? Two of you almost died tonight. I'd prefer not to have to add a detailed explanation as to why someone is dead to my SITREPS."

Tatiana ignored Declan's request and marched right up to Max, who thankfully had holstered his weapon. "Are you okay? How close? Did it graze you? Do you need stitches? Are you bleeding?"

Max's lips twitched. "I'm fine."

"You sure?"

"Yeah. Listen—"

It was like an action movie was playing out in slow motion. I saw it before it happened, was too stunned to warn Max. Tatiana balled her fist up, brought her hand back, and even pivoted her hips to follow through as she punched Max in the stomach. The loud grunt followed by the labored inhale had cut off what I assumed was going to be his apology.

"Glad you're okay. And Declan's right, watch your balls, friend." With a pat on his shoulder, she walked into the house, not sparing a backward glance.

"Goddamn." Max had finally sucked in enough oxygen to speak. "I was gonna say I was sorry," he grumbled.

"Don't think she forgives you." Dec chuckled. "Did you get anything from Nazari's?"

"Yeah. I have the dead guy's phone and gun. Oh, and he's Omni, he had the peacock tattoo. I need to go park the car. I'll fill you in when I get back."

"I'll go with you," Max offered.

"What, you don't want to go into the house yet?"

"Hell, no. She can hit fuckin' hard, bro."

I'd planned on beating the hell out of my friend for being stupid enough to point a gun at my woman. However, true to form, Tatiana took care of it all on her own. Getting gut checked by a woman half your size was way worse than me leaving a few bruises on his face.

We were halfway to where I'd left the car when Max asked, "She really save your life?"

"Fuck, yeah. I was as good as dead."

"Damn."

Damn didn't begin to cover it. I owed her big time.

CHAPTER 27

By the time we'd finished our brief and called Zane to update him on everything that had happened, I was exhausted. Totally and completely drained.

We had more questions than we had answers and we still had two very important missions to execute. Thankfully, the asswipe who had Brooks at gunpoint had felt chatty and mentioned the prince. He'd also called me a bitch. Not that I cared, but knowing Al Issa knew I was in the area and still gunning for him was a tad unsettling.

I was almost to the bedroom when Max stopped me. "You gotta minute?"

"Not tonight."

"Can't wait until tomorrow, Tatiana."

Damn. Fatigue had crept into my bones. I didn't want to have another standoff with Max. I was mentally beat, my guard was down, and I couldn't find the strength to fortify my walls. I couldn't deny his earlier words had cut.

Both before we left and out front when he pointed his fucking gun at me.

"You gonna shoot me now?"

"You gonna kick me in my balls?" he returned.

With a sigh that sounded a lot like something a toddler would make, I turned to face him.

"I was outta line. I'm sorry."

Well, what did I do with his apology? I wanted to be a bitch and tell him to shove it up his ass but again I was too tired to muster the energy.

"I get it. You were right. This is exactly what I was worried about. One of you getting hurt because of me. Nazari and Al Issa both want me dead. Apparently, Leon Brown now wants me dead, too. All of this is my fault. If I'd stayed on my own, none of you would be in danger. Brooks wouldn't have had some asshole's barrel on his head and you wouldn't have had a near miss."

"None of it is your fault. I overreacted. It was…" he trailed off.

"It was, what?"

"Close. Inches. I could feel the wind moving as it went by my face."

"Shit. Max. I'm glad you're okay."

"Yeah. So I'm not excusing my behavior, I was a complete dick. Brooks is gonna rightfully kick my ass. What happened had nothing to do with you and everything about me being a scared pussy."

"Why would Brooks want to kick your ass?" I asked, ignoring the rest. A man like Max wouldn't listen to me if I tried to explain that having a momentary lapse of judgement after having narrowly escaping death didn't make him a pussy, it made him human.

"Babe, I pointed a gun at his woman, who is also a member of this team. You don't do shit like that, and I know better. Good news about Brooks is, when he doles out a beating he expects to be hit back."

Was he nuts? Why was he smiling? Yeah, that's what I was focusing on instead of questioning Max calling me Brooks' woman. It was easier to concentrate on the news the two men would go to blows.

"Are you crazy?" I finally asked. "No one needs to get into a fight. Especially over me. I can handle myself."

"Yeah, babe, you can. I think I have a miniature fist-sized bruise on my stomach. It's a good thing you took me by surprise."

"Why's that? And if you're not careful, you'll have a miniature footprint to match."

"Why is it a good thing you took me by surprise?"

I nodded.

"I didn't have a chance to tighten my abs. If I had, we'd be wrapping up your broken knuckles."

"Pu-lease." I couldn't stop my eye roll. "You wish, tough guy."

"You still gonna kick me in the balls if I promise never to point a gun at you again?"

"Yep."

"Damn."

My grin turned into a smile. I must have been even more worn-out than I'd originally thought.

"What's going on?" Brooks asked, joining us in the hall.

"Nothing," I said.

"We were discussing the future of my testicles."

"Come again?" Brooks frowned and Max smiled.

"My balls. I was asking her what she had planned for them."

"The fuck."

"Stop, Max." I laughed. "He was saying he was sorry and asking if I'd still planned on kicking him."

"We good?" Max asked.

"Yeah."

"Are we?" Max turned to Brooks.

"We will be."

"Right. You two sleep well."

I watched Max disappear down the hall. As soon as he was out of sight, Brooks led us away from the bedroom and toward the bathroom.

"Brooks. I want to get into bed."

"In a minute."

"Brooks."

He turned to face me and before I knew it my back was against the wall and his face was a scant few inches from mine.

"Please, Tatiana. Just give me this."

The look on his face left no room for argument. It was far from anger, not exactly fear, and close to desperation.

"Okay, Brooks."

He closed the door behind us, locked it, turned on the shower, undressed me, then himself, and pulled us under the spray.

He didn't talk, he didn't try to seduce me, though he totally was. He washed my body and my hair. When he was done with me, he quickly soaped up and I found it interesting he washed his hair with bar soap. I'd have to ask him later why he hadn't used shampoo. Much later, when the foul mood of today and this evening had disappeared.

He dried me off and I tried my best to stand still as his strong hands rubbed me down with the terry cotton fabric. He wrapped a towel around his waist and another around me before he grabbed our clothes and walked us back down the hall.

I had to admit, it had been the weirdest shower I'd ever experienced. It had been nonsexual and platonic but I'd never felt more cared for. And his hands running up and down my body sent sparks to all the right places. I couldn't help it. He was hot, and even though he wasn't trying to turn me on, he still did.

We entered the bedroom, and much like the bathroom – minus the locking of the door – he divested me of my towel, walked me to the bed, pulled back the comforter, and waited for me to get settled. All wordlessly. I wasn't sure how I felt sleeping completely nude, but when Brooks leaned down and gently kissed my lips, my brain went fuzzy. When his lips went to my forehead and they lingered there, all thoughts about anything other than Brooks flew out the window.

He however had no second thoughts about being naked. He dropped the towel, picked up two handguns off the small dresser, and walked back to me, setting one on the nightstand next to my side of the bed. A full body shiver had started when he'd first dropped the towel and his tight ass had come into view. The shiver increased to a five-point-five magnitude tremor when he turned and, gloriously nude, he stood in front of me like a warrior beast palming a gun in each hand. *I mentioned naked, right? Completely and totally devoid of clothing. All for my viewing pleasure.* The five-point-five tremor turned into a nine-point-two when he placed *my* gun within *my* reach. He trusted me. Not just a little bit, but with his life.

In that moment, there was not a single thing that he could've done that I would've thought was sexier than him believing in me. Even when I still doubted myself, Brooks believed me to be his equal.

A chuckle slipped out and I quickly covered my mouth to stifle the sound.

"What's funny, Doll?"

"You know, in all the years I was married to James, I'd never allowed him to sleep with a firearm next to the bed. Even before I quit the CIA. When I came home from work, I locked my service weapon in the safe."

"Why?"

"I guess I didn't feel safe with a gun on the nightstand while I slept."

"You know if he wanted to hurt you, he could've."

"I know" I shook my head at the absurdity of my next statement. "It doesn't make sense, but I didn't want to be asleep and vulnerable while he had access to a firearm."

Brooks had unfortunately gotten into the bed next to me, preventing me from continuing to drool over his perfect body. But his sliding next to me, tugging me closer, and settling me against his chest well made up for the loss of sight.

"Did he ever—"

"No. It was about me, not him, really. Forget I said anything."

Brooks was quiet for a long time, which regrettably allowed my mind to wander to James and my shitty marriage. Had it been my fault he'd turned into such an asshole? I thought back over our relationship, tried to find a point in time I'd actually trusted him. Even I could admit the whole gun thing was stupid. He was a SEAL, he knew how to handle a weapon and had argued he could do it better than me. It wasn't that I hadn't trusted him physically, I never thought he'd hurt me. But emotionally, I'd always known he'd demolish me. I knew he'd been hiding something. Yet another time I hadn't trusted my inner thoughts.

"I understand what you're saying," Brooks' whisper cut through the silence. "And I want you to know, I have no problem being asleep and vulnerable with a gun within your reach. As a matter of fact, I trust you'd watch over us."

My hand resting on his chest flexed involuntarily, and if it were possible, I snuggled in closer. He reached down and hitched my leg higher over his thigh and rested his hand near my hip. Our position was intimate. Much different from when the sexual tension was sparking between us and passion was arcing.

"Thank you for saving my life tonight."

"Thank you for saving mine," I returned.

He squeezed me tightly, then relaxed.

As my mind stilled and my eyes drifted closed, it hit me, not once had I thought about my scars.

CHAPTER 28

We'd plotted and planned the entire day. Somehow, Garrett had managed to set up a fake meeting between Nazari and a potential buyer. It was bullshit, of course, but we needed the older shitbag away from the younger shitbag sons and the CIA agent. The woman was still a wild card and it was unclear what her objective was. She was either really good at her job and was seriously committed, or she'd turned. I'd sacrificed a lot for my country, however, I didn't think I could go as far as sleeping with a terrorist to complete my mission. I knew it happened. There were some deep cover agents who did what they had to do to accomplish their objectives. I hoped Ashaki Maloof knew what she was doing and was still on the right side of the fight.

"We're outta here in ten minutes." Declan poked his head into the bedroom.

I'd finished packing up and was zipping up my bag when I answered, "I'm set. Need any help?"

"Nope." Declan's assessing stare settled on me and I braced. "Listen, I wanted to ask you, everything straight with you and Max?"

"We're good." I bit back the rest of what I wanted to say. We'd stay good as long as he never pulled that bullshit with Tatiana again.

"Last night was fucked. I don't agree with what he did. This is not an excuse, but he was hyped up. That first shot that came through the window? It should've taken him out. If he would've exhaled the wrong way, he wouldn't be here. It was unfortunate the two of you walked up when you did. He hadn't even processed he was still breathing. The more I get to know Max, the more I understand his loyalty to this team. I could be wrong, but I think he was pissed because he was worried about you."

He wasn't wrong. Max trusted only us and he'd be the first one to jump in front of a bullet if it meant his team was safe. I also knew why Max didn't trust anyone, but it wasn't my place to tell his story.

"I know you're right. But he knows better than to point a loaded weapon at a friendly. Fuck, accidents happen."

"You're right." Declan turned to leave but stopped and smiled. "For the record, it wasn't loaded, his magazine was empty. He pumped fifteen rounds into the fucker who nearly took his head off. He shook off the shock, jumped off the couch, and before anyone could stop him, he went Rambo. Completely justifiable, the asshole had engaged first. But it wasn't smart the way he reacted."

That was something Declan as team leader was also going to learn. Max was impulsive, but not in a bad way.

He went with his gut and reacted. I'd never known him to be wrong. Until last night. Before I could explain this to Dec, he was already walking away.

I tossed my pack over my shoulder and stared down at the crumpled sheets. I couldn't remember a time I'd slept so soundly on an op. Nor could I remember a woman who felt so good, so right in my arms. I'd been on a wild emotional rollercoaster, complete with twists and turns, peaks and valleys, and upside-down loops since the second I'd laid eyes on Tatiana. It didn't take days for my feelings to change, it took minutes. Sometimes seconds. The fuck of it was, I liked it.

The bottom line was, I simply liked her, more than I should. I'd moved past complicated straight into the daunting task of how I was going to convince her we were right for each other. I wanted her to stay with the team. I didn't know how Zane would react, but neither did I care. He'd have to get over it because she wasn't going back to work for Leon Brown and The Company. I'd handcuff her ass to me before I let her continue to work for a man who'd put her in danger. I also didn't give a shit how mad she got or that it made me a bit of a controlling prick. Her breathing was more important.

I wasn't entirely sure how I'd gotten to this place, but I knew she was the one. I felt it deep in my bones. I didn't know jack about her life before I'd met her, except the few tidbits she'd shared. I didn't know her favorite foods, movies, if she liked to read, her political views. However, it didn't matter. There was a fuck ton I'd need to learn, and I was looking forward to it. For the first time in my life, I wanted to know. And I wanted her to know me, all of me, every dark secret I had.

Everything was moving fast. I was good with that, too. The amount of days I knew her didn't matter. It was what I'd seen in those days that cemented my resolve. I wasn't letting her go. I was going to fight my damnedest to nail her down. There was no other option. I was going to show her I was the man who was meant to walk this life with her.

I took one last look at the bed I'd shared with her, remembering how good she'd felt cradled in my arms. Yeah, I wanted more mornings with Tatiana. Sleepy and soft. Breathy good nights and whispered good mornings.

"Hey. There you are. Zane called in, everything's in place," Tatiana told me as I made my way down the hall. "You okay?"

"Perfect. Why?"

"You're looking at me funny."

"Funny how?"

Damn, she was so hot I wanted to drag her back into the bedroom and start what we hadn't had a chance to do this morning before Thad came banging on the door. Her appeal went way beyond her good looks. There was something in the way she looked at me that made me want to fall at her feet. I was in way too deep for a man who had no idea if she felt anything for him other than physical attraction.

"I don't know. You're just looking at me strange."

"Huh. I don't know, Doll." I stopped in front of her and wrapped my arm around her waist, bringing her flush to my front. "How about you and I go out on a date?"

"A date?"

I had no idea why I'd asked her that. I'd never tried to woo a woman before. Mainly because I'd never been interested in anything permanent.

"Yeah, Doll, a date."

"Um. Brooks, have you forgotten where we are?"

I kind of had, though I wasn't about to admit it to her. I was a highly-trained special operator. I was well-versed in: regroup, improvise, and adapt. Surely I could come up with something.

"I haven't forgotten."

"Then why the hell would you ask me on a date? We're kinda in the middle of something."

"If by *something,* you mean the getting-to-know-you phase, I agree."

"Brooks—"

"Tomorrow night."

"Tomorrow night we're scheduled to recon Al Issa's compound," she reminded me.

"I know."

"If you know, then why would you ask me on a date tomorrow night?"

"Who says some good ole fashioned reconnaissance can't be a date?"

Her eyes flashed, then narrowed. I tried to hold back my humor as her mouth opened and shut a few times before she finally said, "Gee, don't you know how to impress a woman."

"Tell me you don't enjoy scouting secured locations under the threat of physical harm."

Her lips tipped up and she shook her head. "Boy,

you're a real smooth Casanova, aren't you? Promise a girl a little action and she's putty in your hands."

"I'll even let you take point and give you the brand-new pair of NVGs."

"Wow. How can I possibly say no to that?"

"You can't." I lowered my face and nuzzled her neck. Fuck, she smelled good. I'd already been fighting a hard-on as we'd exchanged banter, but as I inhaled her fresh scent, I lost the battle. I pushed our pelvises together and muttered, "And for the record, the action I'm promising won't leave you putty in my hands. It will leave you boneless and exhausted." Her body trembled and I smiled against her neck. "So it's a date?"

"Yeah."

One word laced with so much desire. I groaned into the soft skin under her ear. With a soft touch of my lips, I pulled back and took in her flushed cheeks and glazed eyes. Thank fuck, I wasn't the only one affected.

CHAPTER 29

I was getting ready to jump from the moving SUV. Thad and Max had been droning on about football for the last two hours. Two. We still had four more hours to go.

* * *

UPDATE, the topic had changed to basketball. No less boring and I was still considering throwing myself out of the vehicle. The only good news was, we only had an hour left of the drive. Other than stopping on the side of the road to pee, yes, the side of the road, there were no restrooms in the middle of the desert, we hadn't stopped. I could've gone my whole life without having to drop trou next to a car full of hot men. They, however, had no issue when nature called. They did their business with a smile.

There was one more good part about the drive. Brooks had put his arm around me and tucked me close. I'd dozed off a few times using him as a very hard, very muscular pillow. The ride gave me a lot of time to think. About Brooks, about my life, about where I was going when this mission was over.

There was no way I would be continuing my employment with The Company. I wasn't sure where I was supposed to send that particular resignation letter, but it would be short, very short, two words actually: Fuck Off. Unprofessional, yes. Juvenile and beneath me, yes. I'd considered a more professionally penned notice of my departure, but I figured a death threat was the best I could do and it would be no less-welcomed.

I'd also had time to finally start to process the hurricane that was Brooks Miller. I'd come to a few frightening conclusions: I liked him and I had feelings for him that went beyond sexy fun times. How in the world that had happened I had no idea. It was insanity, but I couldn't deny that when I felt his eyes land on me, my skin heated. His touch overwhelmed me. When he spoke, I felt his words deep in my soul, they soothed my tattered heart. Even though I'd come to the uncomfortable realization I was falling in love with a man, who may or may not want me for more than a roll in the hay, I still had no clue how I was supposed to proceed.

We were in the middle of an op, I was going to be jobless *and* homeless. The last thing I should've been worried about was the way Brooks made me tingle. I shouldn't have been behaving like a giddy schoolgirl with her first crush. And he shouldn't have been flirting and asking me out on dates. I wasn't about to condemn him for the sex we'd had, even though that shouldn't have happened, either. I liked that part, and hoped before everything was over, I could convince him it needed to happen more. There were a lot of *shouldn't haves* swirling around in my head.

I cut my eyes to the handsome man sitting next to me and wondered what was stopping me. He wasn't James. Far from it. Even when James was trying to get me to go out with him, he never made me feel the way Brooks did. They were night and day. My ex was a sweet talker, always trying to bullshit. Brooks was straight with his words and honest with his reactions. He'd never massaged the truth so I would like his answer. I pushed all the red flags that were waving in front of me to the side and decided to throw caution to the wind. I had to see where things would lead with Books. If I didn't let down the walls I'd built to protect myself, I'd regret it.

"Everything okay?" he asked.

"Yeah. Just thinkin'"

"Come to any conclusions?"

"A few."

"Any of those conclusions gonna piss me off?" he asked then leaned in close. "Your death stare doesn't work on me, Doll."

Smug bastard.

"I know it doesn't. You have yet to vanish in a puff of smoke."

His face lit with humor. His hazel eyes danced with mirth. And finally his head tipped to the side and his laughter filled the SUV. Damn, he was hot. Looked even better when he was smiling.

"You're funny."

"I wasn't trying to be."

He was back to invading my space and whispered, "I don't know about the smoke part, but when we're together, you set me on fire."

The eye roll was instinctive and immediate. "You should stop talking."

"Why? You like my mouth." His words were spoken against my skin and when his tongue came out and touched my skin I was reminded how right he was. I did like his mouth.

"You like my fingers, too."

Okay. He had me there.

"But I think there are other parts on me you like more."

What could I say? He was right.

"I think you may need a reminder."

I didn't argue when he told me I needed the reminder even though he was wrong. I didn't need one, but I wasn't so stupid I'd turn down the offer. The times we'd been together were forever woven into my memories. Even if he walked away tomorrow, I'd never forget. Not a single second of it. Not his mouth, not his fingers, not other parts of him. But what I would remember the most was, how he'd given me back something huge. A piece of myself I'd forgotten I possessed—courage. He'd reminded me I was strong and brave. I was smart and good at my job. He'd made me feel sexy, he didn't care about my scars, he embraced them. I was grateful for that, too. But nothing could trump him giving me back my self-worth.

With a masculine chuckle, he righted himself but kept his arm around me. I tried my best to curb the lust he'd built and went back to thinking about our day.

After one last briefing with Zane where he'd confirmed we were mission go, we headed to the meeting location Matek Nazari had been sent to. The smug bastard had been sitting in the outside dining area of one of his favorite restaurants. Kyle had taken the shot. I'd also learned that he was the best of the bunch with a long gun. Though all the guys had bickered, he was only better by less than a fourth of an inch. Which in some cases was the difference between a hit or a miss. Kyle hadn't missed, it was clean and precise, and Matek Nazari was dead.

I should've felt some relief that the man was no longer alive and able to send hitmen after me, but I wasn't. While extinguishing the scumbags of the planet was a necessary evil, I'd never rejoiced in it. Though, once Al Issa was in the ground, I may feel differently. I wanted him dead for personal reasons. They were biblical actually; an eye for an eye. No, he hadn't physically killed me, but a part of me had died while his men carved me up.

Kyle's voice giving Declan directions to the house we'd be staying in pulled me from my thoughts of death and retribution.

"Are you fuckin' sure about this?" Thad asked from the third row of seats where he and Max were sitting behind me.

"You handling nav, or am I? That's right, *I am*. I got the GPS out, asshole." Kyle's outburst was dripping with sarcasm.

Good to know. Everyone was as cranky as I was from the world's most boring road trip across the barren, sandy, desert. There weren't even trees to look at. Nothing.

We passed a sign warning us there were only five kilometers until the Kuwaiti border crossing and Kyle spoke again, "Slow down, the dirt road is coming up in five hundred feet. Turn right."

Declan found the road and slowed even more now that we were back onto a gravel road. Maybe I should back up to the part of the day where travel routes were discussed, and clarify. There was indeed a faster route from Al Qatif to the Raqa'i Port. One that was full of paved interstates and places to stop and eat. However, the team, much to my chagrin, chose the scenic desert route minus the scenery. This was bumpy. It also added two hours to the already five-hour drive. Seven hours sitting in a car had made me crabby, too.

I don't think I'd ever been so happy to see a single level, tan colored, L-shaped… hut? Maybe it could be called that. I wasn't sure what defined a structure as a hut versus a house, but looking at the building, I was leaning toward hut. Nothing about it screamed safe, however my ass was so numb and I had to pee again so I wasn't going to suggest we call Zane Lewis and tell him the accommodations he'd provided sucked.

"We're here," Kyle unnecessarily announced.

Brooks shook his head and smiled. "Ready?"

"God, yes."

If he didn't hurry up and move out of my way, I was going to climb over him to exit.

"Eager, huh?" His eyebrows wiggled, and as childish as his statement was, I couldn't help laughing.

Maybe I was delirious from the mind-numbing ride. Maybe I was eager to sample some more of his hot body and talented tongue. I wasn't sure what I blamed my next move on, but I leaned toward him as he was exiting the car and kissed him square on the mouth in front of everyone.

Nothing like jumping in with both feet and a blindfold on. I prayed I knew what I was doing.

CHAPTER 30

Holy fuck. I was stunned motionless. The shock of her kiss hadn't worn off when Thad's meaty paw slapped my shoulder.

"Move it. I want out of this tin can. And next time, you two lovebirds get the back so I don't have to watch you make out."

"No one was making out," Tatiana protested. "And next time, I'll remember my noise cancelling headset. My ears are bleeding after seven hours of the two of you arguing about deflated footballs and the Lakers' draft pick for the year."

"Wagner is our ticket to a winning season," Thad argued.

"I don't know who that is, and I don't care."

"You four gonna sit in the car all night, or get out?" Declan asked.

I was definitely getting out and so was Tatiana. There'd be payback for the kiss she'd planted on me. The good kind of retribution that would have her panting and begging. I hoped the walls in this piece of shit house were thick because there was no way I was taking it easy on her. Not when I was feeling ten feet tall and like a caveman.

I gripped Tatiana's hand and helped her out of the back seat. Once she was settled on her feet, I went to the back of the SUV to grab our bags. Kyle was already standing watch, Declan was sweeping the perimeter, both had their weapons out, ready for anything. Which reminded me, I gave a sharp whistle and Tatiana turned to look at me. I patted my hip, reminding her she needed her gun at the ready as well. Her Sig cleared her holster and she followed Declan. I knew she was rolling those pretty eyes of hers and if she were closer, she would've given me shit. Yeah, she was feisty, I was damn lucky.

Less than an hour later, we were settled in the house, the perimeter was trip wired, and Declan's crazy ass had set some IEDs around the points of entry. Garrett had called to inform us that he and Tex were able to move all of Matek's money. His sons would be left penniless. They'd never touch the blood money their father had acquired. Instead, the two computer-hacker-geniuses divided up the funds and anonymously donated hundreds of millions of dollars to relief organizations around the world. There was a girls' school in Africa that would have funding for years. A Midwestern state in the US that had counties so poor they were closing schools, were now flush with cash. A town in the state of Michigan that had water issues for years would no longer need to worry about bottled water. The money had gone all over, good people would benefit from his ill-gotten gains. That was the good news.

The bad news was, we were in a holding pattern. Tex had new drone footage of Al Issa's compound and more men had arrived. We were already out-numbered, but it was manageable. With the addition of ten more men, it was questionable. Thankfully, Zane didn't do questionable, so we were going to sit on our thumbs for a few days and see what the prince did.

The extra days and nights I would get with Tatiana were welcomed, but the longer we were in the area, the better the chance someone would see us and tip off Al Issa. Or think it would be a good idea to try their luck at killing a few Americans.

Thad and Tatiana were sitting on the smaller of the two couches, heads together as they looked at her laptop balanced on her knees. My gaze moved lower and something that felt a lot like jealousy started churning in my gut at the sight of their thighs touching. He was casually chomping on a protein bar and she was pointing to something on the screen.

"You look like you're ready to rip someone's head off, buddy," Kyle said and followed my stare.

Thad turned in our direction and shoved the last of his bar into his mouth. He chewed, swallowed, then smirked. Then he moved. Not to get up and stop touching my woman, no not Thad. The fucker stretched his arm closest to Tatiana above his head and in a move every teenage boy in the world had tried, he lowered his arm down behind her and turned closer.

The jealousy rolling around was now threatening to bubble over.

"Great. You woke the sleeping bear," Kyle joked.

"It's not my fault I'm a big man," Thad returned, humor lacing his tone.

"Seriously?" Tatiana finally glanced up from her computer and looked at me.

Thad and Kyle both chuckled, obviously finding humor in my discomfort. If I wasn't the one pissed, I would've been able to see why they'd think it was funny. But I was pissed, so I didn't see anything funny about the game Thad was playing.

"You mind?" I asked Thad.

"Not at all," he said, but made no effort to move.

Irrational annoyance and possessiveness washed over me. I went to take a step toward the couch when Kyle grabbed my arm. "He's fuckin' with you."

I knew he was. That was where my annoyance stemmed from. Tatiana wasn't a game and I wasn't joking. She was mine and no one, not even Thad, was going to touch her.

"Oh, for fuck's sake, caveman. We're looking at maps, not watching porn," Tatiana told me.

"What'd we miss? Who's watching porn?" Max asked as he walked into the room with Declan.

"*Not* watching porn," Tatiana corrected.

"Damn. That's too bad."

Declan remained quiet while he took in the scene, then muttered, "Totally understand Zane now. I owe him an apology and a box of donuts."

"Don't lump us in with the Red Team. Just because

lover boy over there has his panties in a bunch doesn't mean the rest of us are stupid. Zane had to deal with Linc, Jaxon, Leo, and Colin. We are practically monks compared to them." Kyle laughed.

"And don't forget Jasmin. That woman is harder to handle than any man on that team," Max added.

"We're a quiet drive in the park compared to them," Thad told Dec. "Brooks is just jealous his woman would rather sit next to me than—"

"I'm not jealous," I denied.

"Dude…" Kyle trailed off as if all he needed was one word to call me on my bullshit.

"Has anyone gone over the last SITREP Garrett sent over?" Declan thankfully inquired, moving the conversation back to work and away from my newfound jealousy.

"Yeah. We're looking at it now," Thad answered.

"I was thinking," Tatiana started. "We need to watch the black market and bidding. The new additions could be there for transport of goods. If an auction just ended, the buyer could've sent in a convoy to pick up their product. It's not like Al Issa calls UPS for a pick-up to ship and the buyer would never show personally."

"You could be right," Declan conceded.

"Also, if a pick-up was scheduled, Al Issa would have extra guards on the compound. I looked at the historical imagery, it seems when Al Issa visits the compound there are only four outside guards. Tex's intel showed ten perimeter, three in the courtyard, and five on the roof. That's overkill. His compound is literally in the middle of the desert. One rooftop spotter would suffice."

"But if he had millions of dollars of goods to be transferred, he'd up his security," I added, agreeing with her assessment.

"Exactly. He's a pompous prick. He believes he's untouchable. He doesn't even have personal protection for any of his wives."

Tatiana had abandoned her laptop and was pointing to a topographical map that was spread out on a coffee table in front of her. She scooted to the edge of the couch so she could mark points of interest. As much of an ass as it made me, I was happy she was no longer touching Thad.

"He built this compound, though he calls it a palace, of course. Tactically it is perfect. Nothing but miles and miles of bare earth. A spotter would see dust rollin' from a vehicle before the palace walls even came into the driver's view. Less than a mile from the Iraqi border. Easy smuggling, easy day."

I couldn't help the smile that formed. "Now you're getting' it, Doll."

Once the humor of her statement had worn off, something hit me—just how much she'd changed. She'd gone from offended woman to team member. She'd once bitched about alpha males and SEAL lingo and now she was spouting it off herself. She'd thrown a hissy fit over me offering to help her with her bag, accusing me of being sexist, to not uttering a word when last night I brought her stuff into the house for her. Then there was her public display of affection. Not to mention, thus far every kiss we'd shared, I initiated. That was what had taken me by surprise, not that she'd necessarily done it in front of the guys, but that she'd done it at all.

"I think Zane's right. We need to wait this out. After

the transfer he'll send away some of the guards," she finished.

"You and Brooks are still on recon tomorrow night," Declan stated. "Let's hope the tablets aren't what's being transported out."

"They're not."

"How do you know?" Max asked.

"I just do. I feel it. As long as he has those tablets, he knows I'm coming for him. And he wants me dead more than he wants the money from the sale."

"Wonderful," Dec mumbled. "I don't want any hero shit, Tatiana. I even catch a whiff of you thinkin' about going rogue, I'll yank your ass from this op."

She held her hands up in front of her like she was warning off an attack. "Just stating the facts. He's got a hard-on for me. My gut's telling me, he wants to dangle the tablets in front of me thinking he can get me to come to him."

"And that's exactly what we're doing," I pointed out.

"The difference is, now I have you at my back."

There it was. She trusted me, trusted all of us to help keep her safe. I didn't believe for a second that if the opportunity arose, she wouldn't go kamikaze on Al Issa. Not that I could blame her. But personal vendettas clouded one's judgement. I understood her need for retribution, but I wouldn't allow her to die in the process.

CHAPTER 31

"Wake up, Doll."

I opened my eyes and snuggled closer to Brooks. Every muscle in my body was deliciously sore. When Brooks had told me he was going to remind me how much I liked "other parts" of him, he wasn't lying. The second we'd gotten into the bedroom, he set about making sure I'd never in this lifetime forget. Not that I needed the reminder, but again, I wasn't dumb enough to pass up three really great orgasms.

"Morning," I mumbled against his chest.

My hand that had been resting on his pecs near where my cheek was pressed started roaming. *If I was awake, I might as well cop a feel.* He was warm, and smooth, and hard. His chest and abdomen completely bare of any hair. Which was strange because he had thick, dark leg hair that tickled my skin as I rubbed our legs together under the sheet. His forearms also had a smattering of hair, enough that it obscured some of the tattoos he had there. They all were military-related; a flag, eagle, old-style black powder gun, a faceless warrior.

Brooks slowly rolled me to my back. All thoughts of tattoos and lack of chest hair flew out the window as he loomed over me. He brushed my hair away from my face and stared down at me.

"You're so beautiful."

"Thank you," I whispered, still not used to this big, strong, handsome man giving me compliments.

"I think we need to talk."

Without permission, my eyes closed and my body stiffened. Oh, no. How had I read the situation so wrong? We'd agreed neither of us wanted complicated and I'd stupidly allowed myself to start having feelings for him. I was so, so foolish. Why would I ever think a man like Brooks would be interested in anything more than a little fun on a mission? I was easy. A convenient lay. I knew I shouldn't have allowed myself to believe when he told me otherwise.

"Stop." His voice was no longer rough with sleep.

"I'm not doing anything, Brooks."

"Yes, you are. I've lost you again. You've gone back into the fucked-up place in your head where you think the worst."

"It's not fucked-up. We don't need to have any talk. I get it."

"Really? What exactly do you get?"

He nudged my thighs farther apart and settled himself into the cradle of my hips. There was no way I wanted to have this conversation lying in bed naked with him. I needed to be fully clothed and standing. Actually, I preferred to have this conversation never.

I still hadn't answered him when I felt his hand move between us, not stopping until it was between my legs.

"Mm. Wet already," he groaned. "Tell me what you get, Doll."

How embarrassing.

His hand disappeared and the broad head of his dick was now pushing inside of me.

"Do you get that things have changed?"

He pushed in a little more.

"Do you get that shit got complicated?"

He was inching his way inside of me and it was frustrating as hell. I lifted my hips, trying to get him to give me more, but he pulled back.

"Answer me, Tatiana."

"Yes, I get it."

He slammed home and my breath was caught in my throat. Damn, he felt good.

"Why aren't you moving?" I complained.

"Do you get that this got serious before we left Bahrain?"

I was having a hard time comprehending what he was saying.

"What?"

Brooks slowly pulled out and eased back in. Over and over. His unhurried strokes were building something deep.

"I'm not letting you go after this mission is over."

"Okay," I agreed.

"You're staying with the team."

"Okay."

He hadn't stopped moving, not his cock as it tunneled in and out of me. Not his hand on my face that caressed my cheek, and not his other hand that was flexing as he held my thigh.

"Brooks," I panted. "More."

The force of his thrust increased and my orgasm was approaching.

"I'm falling for you," he whispered.

"Okay…What?" I tried my best to focus on his face through my haze of desire. "What did you say?"

He dropped to his elbow, giving me more of his weight. "I said," he started, and kissed my forehead before he continued, "I'm falling for you."

My rapidly-beating heart was now threatening to seize. "What does that mean?"

"Haven't you been listening?" He smiled.

"Um. No."

"I've been talking."

"For future reference, if you want to have a talk where I pay attention and participate in the talk, you shouldn't have it while you're fucking me."

"I'm not fucking you, Doll." Now I was really confused. And the orgasm that had been building was retreating. "This is us, talking about something important while we make love."

"Make love?"

"I'm speaking English, baby."

"I know that—" Brooks slammed into me, cutting off my snarky comment. "Oh, God."

Gone was the leisurely pace. My back arched, my hips lifted to meet him, and my orgasm was racing forward.

"You gonna stay with me?"

"Uh-huh."

"Not good enough." He slowed. "Tell me."

"I'm gonna stay with you."

"I'm not gonna let you go," he warned.

"Okay."

"Tatiana, I'm gonna hold you to it. You're mine."

He pushed his face into my throat and kissed me there. I couldn't help it, I snapped. I loved the feel of his mouth on my skin, his weight and heat surrounding me—overwhelming me. I felt safe and protected. Wanted. Sexy. Loved. My hands groped at his back trying to find purchase, my ankles crossed, and my heels dug into his lower back.

"I'm falling for you, too," I told him.

Brooks went wild. It was fucking beautiful. If this was what he called making love, I prayed he wanted to make it every day. One orgasm broke and his mouth slammed down on mine, swallowing my screams. He didn't stop to give me a second to catch my breath before he started building another.

I wrenched my lips from his and begged, "Baby."

All he did was growl and speed up his pace. Sweet Jesus, I was going to die.

"One more," he demanded. I tried to shake my head no but he wasn't having it. "Come on, Doll. You're close. Just let go."

"I can't." And I couldn't—it was too much. He was

building something big. Way bigger than an orgasm. He was building hope and need. It was too scary.

"I swear. Swear it, Doll, I will catch you. I'm there with you. Let go and fall."

I had a feeling he wasn't just talking about my orgasm, though I couldn't stop that, either. I toppled over the edge, my pussy convulsed and endorphins flooded my system. The pleasure was intense, but the swelling in my heart was bigger.

"Okay, Brooks," I moaned and let go.

Either he'd catch me or I'd fall fifty stories to my death.

Only time would tell.

CHAPTER 32

"Would you stop fucking pacing?" Max grumbled.

"They're late," I reminded him.

"And you wearing a hole in the floor gonna change that?"

I flipped him the bird and continued walking back and forth, stopping in front of the window every few seconds to look out and see if they were back.

Tatiana and Declan had patrol tonight. They'd made the half-mile walk to the small town near the Raqa'i border crossing. They should've been home already. I was unusually on edge. My gut in knots. Something was wrong. I could taste the sour mix of dread and apprehension.

"It's only been ten minutes," he spoke again.

Only? Shit could slide from normal to fucked in less than ten minutes.

I thought back over the last week we'd been in Saudi Arabia. I'd had seven magnificent days with Tatiana. We'd had our recon date, it had been the single best date of my life. Guns, NVGs, a hot chick, and adrenaline. What more could a man want? During the assignment, she'd been the perfect partner. She may have questioned her instincts but I didn't. She was thoughtful in her movements and mindful of our limitations. She was smart. I had to keep reminding myself that she knew what she was doing.

Twelve minutes, now. Fuck.

Declan was with her. He'd protect her if shit went south. He was one of the best in the business. Unless he was taken out first. Goddamn it, why didn't I stop her when she pushed to be on rotation for patrol? *Because she would've had your balls, you idiot.* I could live the rest of my life castrated if it meant Tatiana's fine ass was sitting at home safe.

Every second that ticked by was like a blow to my heart. If I'd thought I was in deep last week when I admitted I was falling for her, I was dead wrong. I hadn't known there was such a thing as abysmal. The depth of my feelings for her were boundless, endless, incalculable. I knew more about her than any other person in my life. Seven nights lying in bed after we'd made love talking about everything and anything. I knew every detail of her life and she knew mine. I hadn't held back anything. She knew all my secrets, my deepest fears, ugly shit I never thought I'd admit to another human being. I'd spilled my guts between learning her favorite food was chicken nuggets from McDonald's and her favorite movie was *A Walk to Remember*.

I wasn't falling for her, I was in love with her. And now she was fifteen minutes late coming home from patrol and a goddamn dragon was breathing fire in my belly. Serious as shit, what had I been thinking? The man who'd had her captured and tortured was six-fucking-miles from us. He'd find nothing but pleasure in carving her up again.

I was getting ready to grab my gear and go in search of them when they walked through the door. I took her in from top to toe and nothing looked out of place.

"Hey." She was beaming and I felt like an asshole. She obviously enjoyed working and there I was thinking about chaining her ass to the bed so she couldn't leave the house. Shit. I was no better than James-fuckstick-Monroe.

"Hey, Dell. How was patrol?"

Max chuckled from the couch and I cut my gaze to him. He'd find my size twelve boot up his ass if he told her I'd been pacing like an animal.

"Boring. Sorry we're late." Declan was giving her the evil eye and I wondered what that was all about. "But I had to make a small detour."

"What kinda detour?"

"The kind that could've gotten us in trouble," Declan mumbled.

"You're a drama queen. No one was going to get into any trouble." She shook her head at Declan and made her way across the room. "I saw a vending machine but I couldn't carry this around the whole night, so we had to go back and get it. It was kinda out of the way. That's why we're late."

"You fuckin' kidding me?" I smiled and took the can of Orange Fanta from her hand. "You went back to get me a can of soda?"

"Not any soda. Your favorite. Can you believe there's a vending machine all the way out here in the middle of nowhere that has Orange Fanta?"

She was amazing. Guilt washed over me. I'd been thinking about how much I hated her on patrol and she was doing something kind and fucking awesome for me. Man, I was a dick.

I tagged her around her waist and hauled her close. "Thank you, Doll."

"You're welcome."

Her smile damn near knocked me on my ass. So beautiful and bright.

"Let's get you to bed, I'm sure you're tired."

Max barked a laugh. "Tired. Right."

"Hold up, Zane's calling." Declan stopped me before I could drag her back to the bedroom and show her some naked appreciation.

After a few clipped one-word answers, he handed Tatiana the phone.

"Hey, Z," she greeted. "What?" Her back went ramrod straight and she said, "Let me put you on speaker so I don't have to repeat everything you say… Yes, I'm sure. Whatever it is you need to tell me, my team has the right to know. I don't have any secrets from them." She rolled her eyes and smirked. "Yeah, you'd like to know the answer to that. But I said, my team, not my boss."

Her boss? Her team? Had she made the decision to stay with Z Corps? Had Zane made her a job offer? She had told me she was not going back to The Company no matter what, but she'd never told me she'd talked to Zane.

"Leon Brown is MIA," she told the room as she put the

phone on speaker. "Go ahead, Z."

"Leon Brown hasn't been heard from for seven days," Zane said.

"Seven? So the day after he set up Tatiana?"

"Yes. And that was exactly what that was. Brown ordered the firing pin be removed."

"Why?" Tatiana asked.

Her question gutted me, there was so much pain in her voice. She started to pull away from me, but I held her closer and refused to let her go.

"Tex and Garrett are still working on the why. I'm gonna owe Tex a kidney by the time this mission is over. Do you know how much he charges? A whack, that's how much."

Tatiana went rigid and I wanted to kick Zane's ass. She had no idea he was joking. No doubt Tex's services were expensive but I also knew Tex had never charged Zane full price. As a matter of fact, he often times didn't charge Zane at all.

"What do you think?" Declan asked Zane.

"I think Tatiana was marked the minute you guys walked into the UN annex. I think he had eyes and ears on her at all times. I think he was worried she was getting too close to something and he needed to take her out."

"You think he's dirty? Part of the Omni?" Max was now standing next to Declan.

"I think he's dirty, yes. Part of the Omni, doubtful. But that doesn't mean he didn't have his hand in Falcon Holdings."

"But I was investigating Lucre on Leon's orders," she reminded Zane.

"Lucre. Not Falcon Holdings. I don't think you were supposed to stumble on that bit of fuckery. Listen, I hate to continuously slam the CIA. Okay, I don't really, but I think the CIA wants Falcon up and running. From a tactical standpoint it makes sense. The devil you know is better than the devil you don't. They knew about Falcon, they can watch the money flow. Leon knew our objective was to sweep up Falcon in our takedown of Lucre. As we dismantle Omni, we're gonna hit as many of their subsidiaries as possible."

"Who do you think took out Leon?" Declan inquired before I could.

This was more of the same bullshit games the CIA played. It always played out like a bad movie. At least they were predictable if nothing else. Though they rarely got it right, always needing someone else to clean up their mess. I understood their main objective was information gathering, however they were quick to tuck tail and run when shit hit the fan. I was happy Zane refused to take contracts from them, he'd been burned and didn't believe in second chances. Not to say we still didn't get caught up in their games, case in point our current situation.

"No one. I think he's gone to ground. Someone's not happy Tatiana's still breathing. Not to mention, the rest of you. He underestimated her, and my team. He's fucked and my guess is on the run."

"Perfect," Tatiana muttered.

"Leon Brown is a pissant. We'll worry about him after you take down Prince Douchebag Al Issa. Your mission's been approved for tomorrow night. Tex is taking the lead on intel. He'll guide you in. Tatiana was right. After the shipment of goods was transferred, only four guards remained. Zero-dark-thirty you're a go."

I waited for Tatiana to perk up a little at confirmation she'd called the play correctly, but it never came. She was folding into herself, arms crossed in a protective gesture, a frown marred her pretty face. The only good sign I saw was she looked pissed. Steely determination shone in her eyes.

"Copy that. We'll be ready," Declan said, not taking his eyes off Tatiana.

"I'll be in touch. Out."

Zane disconnected and no one spoke. I think we were all waiting to see what Tatiana would say or do, but when she remained silent, Max stepped in front of her.

"You should be happy," he told her.

"Happy? A man I trusted tried to have me killed."

"Yep. He sure did. And he would have if you weren't good at your job. Better than he'd thought, which makes you dangerous. In this line of work, dangerous is the best thing you can be. It also means fucktards like Brown are gonna be gunnin' for you. Stay sharp, stay one step ahead, and stay dangerous. Good news for you is, you have the rest of us at your back and a new boss who won't try and kill you."

Max was correct on all accounts and I was happy he'd been the one to point them out to her. Though she didn't seem to believe him.

"Go get some rest. We have shit to do in the morning and it's gonna be a long night tomorrow." Declan slapped Max on the back as he passed. "Max is right, Tatiana. Leon Brown wouldn't have tried to kill you if he hadn't thought you were a threat. The hit proves you're a damn good investigator and a good operator. You should sleep well tonight knowing your instincts are spot on. Let all the other bullshit roll off."

With a chin lift to Max, I tugged Tatiana toward the hall. He'd stay up and take watch until Kyle got up to relieve him. I closed the door behind us and knelt in front of Tatiana, untying her boots and pulling them off. When I stood, she still looked like she was lost in her head. She let me take off her tac vest, her shirt, her pants, and lead her to the bed. Once she was situated under the sheet, I quickly divested my clothes and climbed in next to Tatiana.

"Doll?" I opened my arms and waited.

Without hesitation she curled into my side and rested her arm across my stomach. Damn, she felt good wrapped around me.

"You okay?" I asked.

"Yeah. Just sucks I was so wrong about Leon." There was nothing to say to that, so I just held her and waited. "Something feels off. I can't put my finger on it, and it's driving me crazy. The connection between Lucre and Falcon wasn't hard to find. It took me all of an hour to discover it. It was easy."

"Maybe easy for you. He might've thought it was buried deep enough that the connection wouldn't be found."

"No. I'm telling you it was right there. Payments from Lucre to different warehouses that Falcon Holdings own. It wasn't hidden, anyone could've found it."

"You don't give yourself enough credit, Doll. But say it

was too easy why would Leon want you to find it?"

"That's what's bothering me. I don't think it's the Lucre and Falcon connection that Leon's worried about. I think it's Ashaki Maloof."

"The agent posing as Matek's daughter?"

"Yeah. I mean, all of that was fucked. Nothing makes sense about why he'd pretend she was his daughter. And did he ever really have a daughter?"

"Do you think Leon was protecting Ashaki?"

"Yes. That's the only thing that makes sense to me. I got the kill order as soon as we got back from Nazari's. Zane's right he had eyes and ears on me. He knew what we saw and we'd figured out the woman was not his daughter."

"One problem with that, Doll. The man you shot mentioned the prince."

"Not if Leon sold us out completely and told Al Issa we were in the area. The enemy of my enemy is my friend. Why not let Al Issa do his dirty work?"

Fuck. That made sense. Especially the part about Leon Brown selling us out to Al Issa.

"Doll, as much as I want to lie you out and make love to you, I think we need to wake the guys and tell them what you just told me. If Al Issa knows we're coming for him, we need to shift our mission."

"I know."

She started to roll away but I held her tight. "One more thing. You make a decision about staying with the team?"

"I wanna stay. Are you okay with that?"

"Fuck, yeah. I was trying to come up with ways to

make you not wanna leave."

"Will Zane be okay with…um…"

"Us?"

"Yeah."

I let my eyes drift closed for a second, ridiculously happy there was an "us."

"He'll be fine. Jasmin and Linc are on the same team."

"But they're married."

"And? Where is it you think we're headed?"

"You wanna marry me?" Her words came out rushed.

"This keeps going like it has been, then yeah, Doll, I wanna marry you."

"I've only known you like a minute."

A minute, a day, a year, I knew she was the one. The day I'd walked into the UN annex and met this prickly, smart, beautiful, sexy woman, my life had changed. I'd known it then and wasn't stupid enough to let her go now.

"And?"

"You're crazy." She laughed.

"Crazy about you."

Her body continued to shake with laughter, and as much as I was enjoying her warm body pressed against my side and her happy, we had to get up. The rock that had been tumbling around in my gut was now a boulder. Tatiana was right, something was off, and nothing about Leon made sense. When all of this was over, we were going someplace tropical, with a beach, fruity drinks, and peace. I wanted her all to myself where we could stay in bed all day without the threat of someone trying to kill her. Right after I convinced her to say, I do.

CHAPTER 33

Unfortunately, we'd gotten out of bed and dressed. I would've much rather have stayed where we were but Brooks was right. We needed to talk to the guys. Leon Brown being MIA was a problem. And now that we had confirmation he'd ordered my weapon to be rendered useless, it wasn't a stretch he'd also sold us out to Al Issa.

I'd started to open the bedroom door when Brooks stopped me and pulled me close. God, I loved being in his arms. Loved when he wrapped me tight and looked down at me. I felt loved and protected and that was okay because I knew he believed I could take care of myself. For some reason, that made all the difference. Him respecting me as an equal allowed me to lower my guard. It felt good, something I'd never had before. I didn't have to prove to Brooks I was good enough, he already thought I was.

His head lowered and his firm lips touched mine. It

was a sweet kiss, all too short, the kind that left you begging for more.

"Later when we get back into bed, I'm gonna show you how much I love you."

My world shook. Fireworks sounded. My vision dimmed.

It took me a moment to realize it wasn't his declaration of love that had tilted my universe. The house had literally shook. There were no fireworks bursting in my mind, we were taking heavy artillery. My eyes hadn't clouded over in a haze of joy and happiness, the lights were out and the ceiling was crumbling.

"Fuck. Stay at my back," he ordered.

The only indication he'd opened the door was the creak, it was that pitch-black. I had to shuffle my feet so I wouldn't trip on the broken pieces of plaster on the floor.

"SITREP?" Declan shouted.

"Four out front approaching," Max answered.

I collided with Brooks' back when he came to a halt. "Here."

I fumbled with the helmet that was shoved into my chest, barely keeping ahold of the gun in my hand. I shoved my weapon into the waistband of my cargos, happy we'd gotten dressed before the attack, and strapped the helmet on, fumbling in the dark to pull the night vision goggles down.

It took a moment for my eyes to adjust to the green tint and the room to come into focus. Max was standing to the side of the blown-out window, Kyle standing next to him struggling to tie his boots. Declan was coming into the living room strapping on his vest. Thad had AR15s slung over his shoulder. He dropped the load on the couch and took off back toward the bedrooms.

Declan picked an AR and tossed it in Brooks' direction. He easily snagged the rifle midair and handed it back to me.

Another burst of gunfire splintered the door, bullets whizzing by us in all directions.

"Goddammit!" Declan yelled before he returned fire. "You two cover the back."

"Roger." Brooks turned and started back down the hallway we'd just come from.

Now that I could see the destruction, I was amazed the house hadn't completely collapsed. Not to say it wouldn't at any time. Plaster and other debris crunched under my boots, the odor of spent gunpowder thick in the small house told the seriousness of our situation.

"Take right," Brooks ordered.

Wordlessly, I complied, covering our three o'clock as we approached the bullet-ridden back door. Brooks broke left without a moment to spare. The battered door blew in, exploding into hundreds of pieces of deadly flying shrapnel.

I turned my back to the blast and crouched, covering my head the best I could. Heat from the discharge waned, I stood and turned in time to see the first man enter, the barrel of his rifle aimed at Brooks' prone body. Without hesitation, I pulled the trigger and moved to the man behind him, firing a second round. With my night vision goggles askew from the initial attack on the door, I'd missed the third man. The wind was knocked out of me right before hot, searing pain radiated through my left arm. I stumbled back, lost my footing, and landed on my ass with a bone-jarring thud.

This was it, this was how I died, on the floor of a ramshackle house in the middle of the Saudi desert, never telling Brooks I loved him back. Fuck. This couldn't be it. This was not how I was going to let our story end. I had to pull my shit together, not fighting would be suicide. With great effort, I lifted my AR. More gunfire exploded. Mine and his. Both bullets tore through flesh, mine pierced his throat, his hit my leg. Red liquid soaked my clothes as blood freely flowed from my gunshot wounds. The pain was near-crippling. Neither would stop me from getting to Brooks.

It was a miracle I'd gotten to my feet at all, but once I did, I wished I'd crawled. I could've moved faster if I'd stayed on my hands and knees. With awkward, jerky strides, I got to Brooks. Blood was covering his face and for a moment I was afraid I was going to throw up. The bitter scent of smoke and blood mingled together into a pungent smell that threatened to take my breath.

The guys were still taking gunfire from the front of the house. If I didn't move Brooks to safety we'd both die. At least I hoped he was still alive. He wasn't moving and there was so much blood pooling around him, I wasn't sure what was his, the three dead men's, or mine. It all was mixing together in a brew of demise.

Balanced the best I could on my good leg, I reached down and found the grab drag handle on the back of Brooks' tactical vest and prayed to all things holy I had the strength to move him.

"Come on, Brooks, move." I yanked as hard as I could and staggered before I caught my balance.

He'd only moved a fraction of an inch, but it was something. It was going to take an act of God, he was so much bigger than me, and my leg was screaming in pain. The team was engaged in a firefight, I was Brooks only chance. *Our* only chance. Even if I yelled for help, I doubted the guys would've been able to hear me over the barrage of bullets being exchanged.

Ten feet, I just had to get him back into the hallway. On an exhale, I pulled and he slid. With a strength I hadn't known I possessed, I continued to pull. We inched our way down the hall. It seemed like it took forever, I was exhausted by the time I felt it safe enough to stop. It wasn't as far as I'd wanted to take him, but at least we weren't in the doorway anymore. It may've taken minutes, or it may've taken an hour. I had no perception of time. I was fucked, completely and totally screwed. My vision was blurring, and I was getting lightheaded. I needed to check Brooks' injuries, but I knew if I tried to kneel beside him, I'd never get up. The only thing that was keeping me alive was adrenaline and it was quickly waning.

"I'm so fucking sorry, Brooks!" I screamed in frustration.

There was nothing left for me to do. I didn't have enough energy to pull the combat gauze or the Wound-Stat from my vest. Either of those would at least slow the bleeding in my leg. All I could do was keep my AR trained toward the back door and shoot anyone who tried to enter.

"I love you," I whispered.

A cold chill raced down my spine – what if Brooks was already dead, what if he was waiting for me on the other side? What if I just closed my eyes for a second? What if—

CHAPTER 34

I was in the seventh circle of hell. It had been five hours since I'd lost sight of Tatiana. She had been hanging onto life by the thinnest of hairs as she was rushed into surgery.

When I'd come to, Max and Thad were working on her injuries and Declan was performing CPR. If she pulled through, it would be because of them. And Tex. Not me. I'd laid there passed out while my woman was bleeding out, slowly dying, as she protected me. Max, Thad, and Declan had saved her life for obvious reasons, and Tex because he'd been watching the area using drone footage and saw the attack. He was able to call in backup and a medivac. If it weren't for him, she would've died right there on the floor of that fucking house. With me watching, too stunned to do a goddamn thing.

"It's Tex," Declan announced, holding his phone out.

We had the small waiting room at the North Armed Forces Trauma Center all to ourselves. The food Kyle had gone out to get remained untouched on the small table. The team was surviving on coffee and energy drinks.

"Go ahead. You're on speaker."

"First, I wanted to tell you I dialed into the hospital's database. There're no updates, but I'll keep checking." That was a nice way of saying he'd hacked into the hospital records. "There's a Delta team ready and waiting for my go-ahead. Shit time to ask, but I have to know. Should I give Ghost the green light or are you going back in?"

His question was a punch to the gut. Another reminder we'd failed our mission. Al Issa was still breathing, even if the small army he'd sent to take us out weren't. I'd never forgive myself for letting my team down. While they'd been battling for their lives, I was of no help. Truth be told, I was the weak link. I could've gotten them all killed. Tatiana had covered the rear of the building, only finally laying her gun down when the last man was dead.

The team had told me when they came into the hallway, she was standing over me; sheet white, panting, arm shaking, holding her AR. But she'd not given up. It wasn't until Declan told her they were clear that she had dropped. Literally, like a ton of bricks, she just collapsed.

She was a motherfucking warrior queen. A hero. And I hated myself that she'd had to be one because my pansy ass was asleep.

Fuck.

Now another team was on standby to finish a job we should have completed. No, Tatiana should have the pleasure of doing. She deserved the honor of removing Al Issa from the face of the earth. He'd wronged her.

But she'd never get that option.

"Send in Ghost's team," Declan instructed Tex.

"What?" I turned from the window I'd been mindlessly staring out to face Dec.

"This is ours," I reminded him. Suddenly an irrational thirst for blood rose up. The need to maim and kill was overwhelming.

"Being here is more important. Tatiana is more important."

"Taking out the man who put her here is important," I returned.

Declan leveled me with a stare that could only be described as demonic. It looked like the devil himself had graced us with his presence.

"Al Issa will be put down like the pig he is. It just won't be us who sends him to hell. You're needed here, we all are. I'm not leaving my teammate, not even to avenge her. You feel like you gotta be the one to take him out, I won't stop you. I'm sure Ghost would have no problem with you joining him and his team. But I'm gonna warn you right now, that fire you feel in your belly, that desire to kill for pleasure is a dangerous path to go down. It's a stain that never goes away. You have two options, but there is only one right choice."

"I already got hashmarks on my soul. What's—"

"Bullshit. Don't dishonor what we do. We protect. We serve. We are selfless, not self-fulfilling. You go out there right now and take him out, it will be for one reason only. And it will not be for the betterment of humanity. That's all we have, brother. In our line of work, we take the hashmarks but we do so with a clear mind and a clear heart. Morally sound. Once you take that shot in hate, you're no better than them." Declan stopped and took a deep breath and shared. "I know because I live with it every day."

That was the most personal information Declan had ever shared. I stood eyeing my friend and wondered what he'd been through, and if I could live with myself if I wasn't the one to dole out retribution. But the one thing I did know was, if Tatiana woke up and I wasn't here with her, that would be unforgivable. She'd sacrificed herself to keep me safe. My place was by her side.

"Send in Ghost," I told Tex.

"Good call. I'll let them know and keep you updated."

"Thanks." Declan's voice was still gruff. He was locked away in some memory I was sure he wished he could forget.

"And, Brooks?"

"Yeah?"

"There's one thing I know about Tatiana Jones. She's as tough as they come. She's gonna pull through this. I'm just sorry I couldn't get anyone there faster."

"You saved her life. The guys were keepin' her breathin' the best they could but she was gone when the medevac got there. Dec couldn't get her back. Not without the AED. If she lives through this, it will be because you were watching. Thanks isn't enough." I was barely choking out the words, remembering Declan trying to get her heart to beat.

"Never need to thank me for having your back. I gotta make some calls. Out."

Tex disconnected and silence ensued. What was I going to do if Tatiana didn't make it? It was hard to believe I'd only met her the month before. It was like my life before had never mattered. I was happy, going through the motions, but I'd never known love. What it was to love and be loved. I wouldn't survive if she didn't make it.

"She's gonna—"

"Don't say it." I cut off Kyle. "You heard the doctor. She's lost too much blood. He said to be prepared for the worst case."

"Yeah, the man had no bedside manner whatsoever. He also said he'd seen worse and had been successful. You, me, and Thad gave blood, she has enough. You can't give up."

Giving up wasn't in my DNA. It wasn't who I was. I'd never quit anything in my life. The last thing I would ever do was quit Tatiana. But I was fast running out of hope.

CHAPTER 35

"You look damn good for a woman who died three different times."

Before I could volley a comeback to Zane, Brooks growled.

"Too soon?" Zane laughed.

"Yeah, too soon," he answered.

"It's been like three months," Zane reminded him.

"It could be three years or thirty years and it'd still be too soon."

I closed my eyes and tilted my head up, relishing the warm Southern California rays. I'd never thought I'd step foot back into San Diego. I'd left embarrassed, with my tail tucked between my legs. Actually, I didn't leave so much as I fled. As soon as my divorce was final, I packed my stuff into a storage unit and got out of Dodge.

Now I was back, even if only for a few days. Commander Storm North had requested a meeting with the team. NCIS and the FBI had already closed the case on now-deceased Captain Isaac Chambers, the man the Bitoo brothers had been working with. We had been correct, the Bitoos had doubled-crossed Lucre and gone out of the auction. The mistake had cost them their lives. They'd thought they'd keep the holding fee Al Issa had paid them and they'd get a cut from Captain Chambers once the tablets were sold.

"Zane," Ivy, Zane's wife, scolded. "It's not funny."

"I wasn't trying to be funny. I was giving her a compliment. Everyone's so sensitive."

Before Brooks could defend himself, I jumped in. "Thanks, boss, glad you noticed."

Zane smirked and I knew he was getting ready to piss me off, or Brooks. He only got that gleam in his eyes when he was gearing up to be a sarcastic asshole. "You ready to start earning your keep? After months on my payroll, I've yet to get my money's worth out of you."

God, he was a jerk. Or at least that's what he wanted everyone to think. When I woke up after my surgery, he'd been sitting by my bed with the rest of the team. As soon as I was stable enough to move, he demanded I be taken to Germany for recovery. My team never left my side. Then there was Brooks. My guardian. He'd stood watch over me like a sentry. He'd been loving and patient.

Zane had put the Omni case on hold, I guess this was his way of telling us we had work to do. "I've been ready. You're the one who ordered me on bedrest. Not that I've minded." I wagged my eyebrows for emphasis and Ivy laughed.

"She's not—"

"I am, Brooks. And you know I'm right. I was cleared

two weeks ago. We have a mission to carry out. And I need to get back into the fight."

"But—"

"Wasn't it you who reminded me how strong I was? You who told me I was brave? Don't take that away from me. So what, I have two new scars. A wise man told me to wear them proudly. I'm ready."

"You're right." He pulled me close and tucked me under his arm. God, I loved when he did that.

"Great. We done with the touchy feely shit? We got work to do."

Ivy rolled her eyes at her husband. "He likes touchy feely shit. He just pretends he doesn't."

"Ghost's team hit pay dirt when they found Al Issa's laptop." Brooks went solid at Zane's reminder. He was still struggling with what he called a failed mission.

In the beginning, when I woke up and was told a Delta team had been sent in to take out the man whom I felt was supposed to be mine, I'd felt cheated. I wanted to be the one who ended his miserable life. Brooks had thought I'd be disappointed in him that he hadn't exacted revenge. Why he'd thought that, I had no clue. He chose me. Instead of leaving and completing the op he stayed by my side and had been there when I came out of surgery. He was the first thing I saw when I'd opened my eyes after my heart had stopped beating three times.

I was grateful Ghost and his team were able to finish what we'd started. The first step in the destruction of Omni was complete. And with the intel they'd found at the prince's palace, Tex and Garrett had been able to piece together more of the puzzle. Militrix and Lucre were both dismantled. Zane had decided to leave Falcon Holdings untouched. We'd all agreed they held the answers we needed.

"You're headed to Mexico," Zane told us. "But before you head out, I was hoping you could talk to your friend, Faith, at the animal rescue. See if she can give you any insight into how these dogfighting rings work."

"I can't believe we're looking into dogfighting." Kyle shook his head. "I would've never believed there're millions of dollars running through underground fights."

"And where there's illegal money, there are men who don't want to lose their piece of the pie. These men aren't to be underestimated," Zane warned.

"Is that Rocco?" Max cut into the conversation.

We all turned to look. A man was walking across the parking lot with a woman tucked close to his side. Much like how Brooks held me.

"Yeah, that's him." Brooks belted out a loud whistle and I cringed.

"Damn. Warn a woman, would you?"

"Sorry, Doll." Brooks kissed the top of my head just as I knew he would. He was predictable if nothing else.

Rocco glanced up, but not before he stepped protectively in front of the woman, hiding her from our view. The men chuckled as if they weren't the same kind of men. I'd never seen Ivy more than a foot away from Zane, he was always near her, ready to jump in front of her if the need were to arise. And Brooks? He was as caveman as they came. His attentiveness went beyond societal politeness, it knew no bounds. And I was all right with that.

"I heard you guys were in town. I was hoping we'd run into you. This is my girlfriend, Caite McCallan," he proudly introduced.

This was the famous Caite. The woman who had single-handedly rescued three SEALs and had started the domino effect that had caused Captain Chambers' plan to unravel. Good for her. And by the looks of it, she'd caught herself a good man out of the ordeal.

More introductions were made and pleasantries exchanged when Rocco spoke again. "If you guys aren't busy, there's a barbeque down at the beach tonight. Every couple of months—"

"Yeah, I know what happens every couple of months. I just got done reading the SITREP from your last beach party. While I think that a little shootout at what's equivalent to a company party is perfectly acceptable fun, even I'm not—"

"Goddammit, Zane. You're scaring her," Ivy admonished. "I apologize on my husband's behalf. He's been hit in the head too many times." She was talking to Caite but then looked at Rocco. "We would love to join you at the beach. Zane has promised me a vacation out of this trip. We'll start tonight."

"I'm not scared of him." Caite waved her hand in Zane's direction.

What had started out as a few chuckles from the guys turned into an all-out roar of laughter.

"Great. Just perfect. I'm losing my edge. Baby, you have got to stop telling people not to be afraid of me," Zane grumbled.

He was so full of shit.

"Do I know you?" Caite asked me. "You look familiar."

"We actually met in Bahrain."

"Yes. When I was arranging the job fair." She was correct. I'd gone to check out the museums that would be attending, hoping to find new leads on artifacts.

"Good memory."

"So, we'll see you tonight?" she asked.

"Absolutely."

A picnic on the beach sounded awesome. Tomorrow we had a full day planned sorting through the contents of my old life. It was time to junk the past.

"Come on, *ma petite fée.* Time to go home."

Rocco smiled down at Caite as a pretty blush graced her cheeks.

"I think it's time we go home, too," Brooks whispered.

Damn, I loved the sound of that. Home with Brooks. Even if home was a hotel room.

CHAPTER 36

"The sunset is beautiful," Tatiana said from beside me.

We'd broken away from the crowd and had walked down by the water. I had something I wanted to talk to her about, but now that I had her alone, I wasn't sure how to start.

"It is," I agreed. "Do you know how much I love you?"

She turned in my arms, looked up, and her beautiful smile faded. "What's wrong?"

"Nothing. Why would anything be wrong?"

"I don't know. You sound so serious, and your face…"

"What's wrong with my face?"

"Nothing. I mean, you just look thoughtful."

"Thoughtful?" Damn. I was fucking this up. She'd gone from smiling and relaxed to on guard. Not the way I'd wanted this to go. "Tatiana…"

"Are you…breaking up with me?" she whispered.

"Fuck, no. I'm trying to ask you to marry me."

"Marry you?"

I was such a dumbass. I'd ruined everything I had planned. I'd spent hours silently rehearsing what I wanted to say. I wanted this to be perfect for her.

"Yeah, I want—"

"Yes."

"What?"

"Yes, I'll marry you."

"I had this whole speech prepared. I was going to get down on my knee and everything."

"I don't need you to get down on one knee. I don't need a speech. I already know. I don't need words from you, Brooks. You show me every day how much you love me. So, yes, I want to marry you."

My lips twitched at the vehemence of her statement. I was happy she knew how much I loved her. I'd spend the rest of my life making sure she never forgot. "Would you even like the ring? Or is that not necessary, either?"

"Oh, I want the ring." She smiled.

I reached into my pocket and pulled out the jewelry box. The guys had helped me pick it out. When I opened the box, I heard her swift intake of breath.

"Oh my God, Brooks, it's perfect."

I contemplated going bigger, but knowing Tatiana, this was pushing what she'd wear.

"The guys helped." I admitted, pulling the ring from the box. I reached for her left hand and started to slide it down her finger. "The center diamond is us, me and you. But there are four sapphires surrounding us. Our team. They've promised to have our back. Through thick and thin, they'll be there. Always watching."

"I love it. All of it."

I heard the clapping and shook my head. They just couldn't stay away. I should've known better.

"Congrats," Declan started.

"Damn, lucky man," Max said.

Kyle patted my back and Thad pulled Tatiana in for a hug. I should've been irritated I hadn't even had the chance to kiss my soon-to-be-wife before the guys interrupted. But I wasn't. These were my brothers. They'd been there for every important event in my life. It was only fitting they were here for this, too.

"Do you like your ring? I picked it out," Thad told her.

"No, you didn't, asshole. I found it," Max corrected.

"It was my idea in the first place," Kyle put in.

I gave zero fucks the guys were all taking credit for what was my idea. Not when she was standing in the middle of four men who had taken her in and loved her damn near as much as I did. I knew how they all felt about her. Declan had breathed life into her. Thad and Kyle had all given their blood to save her. She was a part of all of us.

"I thought that was you." I heard a male voice from behind me.

I didn't bother to turn, Tatiana's face said it all. She was red-hot pissed. I debated whether or not I should pull her behind me and tell the dickwad to get lost or if I should let her. She squared her shoulders and set her jaw.

Alrighty then, she'd handle it.

"James. How nice to see you." The sarcasm couldn't be missed.

I finally turned and there was James Monroe. He had a pretty blonde girl who had on far too much makeup standing next to him. He was holding her hand and smiling like he'd won some sort of prize.

"I didn't know you moved back."

"I haven't. Listen, Monroe, great of you to come over and say hello but we're a little busy if you wouldn't mind."

"I see you're the same bitch you've always been."

"The fuck you just say?" I growled.

The rest of the team closed ranks. Tatiana put her hand up and shook her head.

"Baby, he's so not worth it. For years, I stupidly put up with him taking his insecurities and failures out on me. It took him a long time and a good amount of verbal abuse *and* cheating to convince me I was the person he'd said I was. A stupid, good-for-nothing bitch who didn't know how to please her husband. But it took you only minutes to remind me I am none of those things."

I took in her words and let them soak deep. Minutes. That was all it had taken.

"Verbal abuse? Sorry if your sensitive panties bunched when I told you the truth about yourself."

"Right. Well, I'd love to say it was nice seeing you, but that'd be a lie. You should probably take your woman and be on your way. There's only so much I'm going to be able to do for you before Brooks decides he's had enough of breathin' your filth. I'd advise you to go now before you're embarrassed."

I'd already decided I'd had enough of her breathing the same air as her ex. She was putting on a good game, but I knew it still hurt seeing him.

"Brooks? Is that your new victim? Sweet as apple pie

until you nail her down. But once she's in your bed, you'll learn you better look elsewhere, you wanna get off."

Before I could beat the holy fuck out of this douchebag for disrespecting my woman, a new voice boomed.

"Monroe!"

It was comical the way James dropped the girl's hand and snapped to attention. The icing on the cake was watching all the blood drain from his face as Commander North stepped in front of him.

"Sir. I was—"

"I heard what you were doing. And believe me, nothing would make me happier than turning my back and allowing these five men to teach you some respect. The only reason why I'm not is because I don't believe the lesson would stick. You're a pompous prick and a disgrace not only to the uniform but the Budweiser. I'm going to rectify both of those immediately."

"I haven't—"

"Listen up, boy. There are a lot of things that can be overlooked. A man disrespecting a woman, no. A man cheating on his wife, never. A man belittling his wife, absolutely not. You've done all three. I proudly command the finest group of men the United States Navy has to offer. You are not a man, you are a cowardly pissant. I don't command those. I will not allow you in my ranks. Consider yourself court martialed. I'll have your article 15 drawn up this evening. The only choice I'm giving you is to turn and leave. You don't, you'll spend the night in the brig."

Unfortunately, Monroe decided to leave without the lesson I was hoping to dole out.

"I'm sorry, Tatiana," Commander North said. "I wish you would've gone to the chain of command so we could've taken care of this."

"I don't believe in meddling in a man's career, sir. I just wanted out, so I left."

"Believe me when I tell you, you would've been doing the Training Command a favor. They've been looking for a way to chapter him out for a long time. It is men, and I use that word loosely as I am in polite company, like him, that can ruin a platoon. Real men don't like liars and cheats. And if he can stab his family in the back, he can sink one into a teammate. You're a lovely woman, you've found yourself a real man."

It was a little funny listening to Commander Storm North trying to check his vocabulary in front of Tatiana. I knew what he really wanted to call James Monroe. But he was old school. A gentleman. A great commander. He would never use coarse words in front of a lady.

"Thank you, sir."

"Enjoy the rest of your evening."

The commander left, and before I could speak, Tatiana did. "That felt great." She beamed. "Nothing like taking out the trash. Thanks for letting me handle it. Though I admit, I was hoping he was going to disobey Commander North. I really wanted to watch you beat him up, baby. I was gonna cheer you on from the sidelines and everything."

Well, I had been wrong. Just when I thought there was nothing Tatiana could say that would surprise me, she went and did it. I'd thought there would be some residual hurt, but there was nothing. Not my woman. She was strong, and tough, and courageous, and so damn beautiful I couldn't wait to get her home. But that would have to wait. There was a party going on and I wanted to show off my future wife.

"How long you gonna make me wait before I get to slip my wedding band over that engagement ring?" I asked as we walked back to the party.

"A few years, at least," she said, shrugging her shoulders.

"Years?" I pulled us to a stop.

The mask of innocence she was wearing started to slip and a wicked smile tugged at her lips. "Damn, you're easy to rile up. I'd marry you tonight, baby."

"Is that so?" A plan was forming. "When are we leaving for Mexico?"

"Forty-eight hours," Declan answered.

"Righteous. Who's up for a road trip?"

"Vegas?" Kyle asked.

I nodded but never took my eyes off Tatiana's face. I wasn't calling her bluff. I was a man who knew what I wanted, and if she was serious, she'd be my wife before the end of the night.

"I vowed never to take another road trip with you all. Last time it was a near-death experience for me." She smiled.

"Nothing bad happened," Max complained.

"You and Thad talked about sports for seven hours. The only thing that stopped me from throwing myself from the car was I hadn't updated my will and I was afraid my bank account would go to fuckstick Monroe."

"Who's going to Vegas?" Zane cut in.

"We are. We're getting married," I told him.

"Christ. I better expand the fucking daycare center I'm being forced to build at the office. Can't anyone just use regular babysitters? Or better yet, birth control?"

"You are so full of shit, Zane Lewis, I've seen you with your nephews. And what about you? You ever heard of birth control?" Tatiana gestured to a pregnant Ivy.

"Ouch," Zane mumbled and looked down at his wife. "Mark this, woman. I'm keeping track, and after you pop my son out, I'm bending you over my lap and spanking you for every time you've pinched me over the last six months."

Holy shit, Zane was having a boy. The world better brace. There was no doubt Lewis genes would prevail.

"Well, what are we all still standing around for? You wanna get married or what?" Zane tapped his foot with impatience.

"You ready to become Mrs. Miller?" I asked Tatiana.

"Hell, yes."

"Let's roll."

CHAPTER 37

Thad

I was seriously questioning my life choices. It had been three days since I'd drunk way too much while celebrating in Vegas. Three days, and the headache was still present. Throbbing behind my eyes like someone was pounding a drum in my skull. The heat and stench of fermenting garbage wasn't helping.

Zane hadn't felt an ounce of pity when he sent us down to Mexico only a day after Brooks and Tatiana had said, 'I do.' The fucker had drunk as much as the rest of us, yet he woke up the next day bright-eyed and bushy-tailed, barking orders like he hadn't polished off a bottle of Knob Creek himself.

Now he and his wife, Ivy, were enjoying something she called a babymoon. *Whatever the fuck that is.* All I knew was, I was walking down Avenida Revolucioń with Max by my side and my Gator sunglasses were doing not a damn thing blocking out the bright rays of the afternoon sun.

Even the brightly-colored buildings were pissing me off.

"You need an attitude adjustment," Max complained. I gritted my teeth in an effort not to tell him to fuck off.

It wasn't his fault I was in a bad mood. Hell, I didn't even know why I was annoyed. We'd all had a great time in Vegas and we'd been stateside for nearly three months. It was the longest I'd been out of the sandbox in recent memory. Maybe that was what my problem was. Three months was a long time to go without a purpose. But that didn't explain my piss poor mood now. We were back on the hunt. Tex had picked up a trace on Leon Brown. It wasn't a great lead but it was a start. Brown had been seen in Venezuela with a woman. With any luck it would be Ashaki Maloof. Though I had a feeling, being CIA she'd be in the wind and back undercover in no time. And as much as I hated loose ends and not fully understanding who she was and what role she played, she wasn't our mission. Omni was. And even if we hadn't been the ones to take out Prince Al Issa, he was dead. Soon Omni would be scrambling.

I needed to snap out of it and get my shit sorted. It may've been broad daylight but there was nothing particularly safe walking the streets of Tijuana. Statistically, I was safer taking a stroll in Kandahar. At least according to OSAC.

"You think Zane put us up in a lime green house just to be a smartass?" I asked Max as we arrived at the Cantina National.

I'd never seen a color so bright on a house in my thirty-two years. It was like a huge neon beacon flashing, alerting all of the homeboys on the block of our presence. We might as well hang a sign outside, too: White boys staying in the lime green house.

"Probably. Something he would do. The color is obnoxious. But it blends into the neighborhood. The one next door is flamingo pink. He coulda put us in that one."

A pretty brunette with long shiny hair cascading to her waist greeted us. She was stunning. And young. Way too young for me to be ogling. Maybe that was part of my problem. It had been a very long time since I'd had the pleasure of anything other than my hand. So goddamn long I couldn't even remember the last time I had female company.

"This okay?" the woman asked.

"Yes. Thank you."

I sat at the table the hostess had guided us to and was grateful Max had been paying attention.

"Earth to Thaddeus." Max knocked on the table, pulling me from my depressing thoughts.

I felt it before I heard it.

A crackle of energy. High-frequency, high-voltage, alternating current. I remembered that feeling. There had only ever been one person who could evoke the phenomenon. Her touch was like my own personal bolt of lightning.

I finally turned toward the clatter of dishes and had to do a double-take. I blinked and tried looking again. The mirage remained, the same beautiful woman at the next table over was staring at me. Green eyes wide in shock and full, kissable lips pulled down into a frown.

She quickly schooled her features and looked back at her lunch companion.

What the fuck?

Max lifted his chin in a silent question, asking if I knew her.

The answer was complicated. Did I know the well put-together woman sitting there eating lunch with a man in an expensive, perfectly pressed suit, donning a watch that cost a year's salary, and douchey haircut that would put you back a whack? No, I did not know *that* woman.

Did I know Emerson Pierce? Intimately. I'd spent hours getting to know every inch of her. That seemed like a lifetime ago. A silly young man who was so stupid he'd mistaken phenomenal sex with love. It had been more than a decade since I'd seen her. I was twenty-two. The sex couldn't have been as good as I'd remembered. Back then, I was so inexperienced I'd probably embarrassed myself. It couldn't have been that great for her, she'd walked out on me.

Emerson stood and straightened the hem of her stylish short red dress and briefly glanced in my direction. Her pretty eyes weren't dancing with desire and lust like they had been the last time I'd been lost in them. They were pleading. She shook her head ever so softly, begging me not to acknowledge her. A part of me wanted to stand and demand answers. But I remained in my seat, not drawing any attention to the fact I could still recall every breathy moan, every groan she made while she rode me. I could still feel her hands in my hair, pulling as my tongue thrashed between her legs. She was a wild thing. Totally shameless in her quest for pleasure.

Her expensive heels clacked on the worn wooden floor as she made her way past our table. If I'd thought the front of her skin-tight dress showed off her curves, it had nothing on the back. Not only did it hug her ample ass but it exposed the smooth skin of her back. My eyes were eating up every sexy inch until they stalled on the thick black lettering of her tattoo.

The last word I'd use to describe the lettering would be feminine. It was bold, going from shoulder blade to shoulder blade, the characters unmistakably Greek. The name unmistakably mine.

Θεοδωρος.

She had insisted on calling me Thaddeus. She said it was strong and sexy, just like I was. She said she'd never forget it. Seemed she was telling the truth.

"You okay?" Max asked.

"Not even a little bit."

For the second time in my life, Emerson Pierce had rocked my world.

*

Emerson and Thad coming soon.

ABOUT THE AUTHOR

Riley Edwards is a bestselling multi-genre author, wife, and military mom. Riley was born and raised in Los Angeles but now resides on the east coast with her fantastic husband and children.

Riley writes heart-stopping romance with sexy alpha heroes and even stronger heroines. Riley's favorite genres to write are romantic suspense and military romance.

Riley Edwards Newsletter –
https://www.subscribepage.com/RRsignup
Add Riley Edwards on Goodreads
http://geni.us/goodreadsre

facebook.com/Novelist.Riley.Edwards

OTHER BOOKS BY RILEY EDWARDS

AVAILABLE ON AMAZON

The Red Team

Nightstalker

Protecting Olivia

Redeeming Violet

Recovering Ivy

Rescuing Erin

The Gold Team

Brooks

The 707 Freedom Series

Free

Freeing Jasper

Finally Free

Freedom

The Next Generation

Saving Meadow

Chasing Honor

Finding Mercy

Claiming Tuesday

The Masters Collection

The Awakening

The Collective

Unbroken 1 & 2 – Season One

Trust – Season Two

Standalone

Romancing Rayne

There are many more books in this fan fiction world than listed here, for an up-to-date list go to www.AcesPress.com

You can also visit our Amazon page at: http://www.amazon.com/author/operationalpha

Special Forces: Operation Alpha World

Denise Agnew: Dangerous to Hold
Shauna Allen: Awakening Aubrey
Shauna Allen: Defending Danielle
Shauna Allen: Rescuing Rebekah
Shauna Allen: Saving Scarlett
Shauna Allen: Saving Grace
Brynne Asher: Blackburn
Jennifer Becker: Hiding Catherine
Julia Bright: Saving Lorelei
Julia Bright: Rescuing Amy
Victoria Bright: Surviving Savage
Victoria Bright: Going Ghost
Victoria Bright: Jostling Joker
Cara Carnes: Protecting Mari
Kendra Mei Chailyn: Beast
Kendra Mei Chailyn: Barbie
Kendra Mei Chailyn : Pitbull
Melissa Kay Clarke: Rescuing Annabeth
Melissa Kay Clarke: Safeguarding Miley
Samantha A. Cole: Handling Haven
Samantha A. Cole: Cheating the Devil
Sue Coletta: Hacked
Melissa Combs: Gallant

KaLyn Cooper: Rescuing Melina
Liz Crowe: Marking Mariah
Jordan Dane: Redemption for Avery
Jordan Dane: Fiona's Salvation
Riley Edwards: Protecting Olivia
Riley Edwards: Redeeming Violet
Riley Edwards, Recovering Ivy
Nicole Flockton: Protecting Maria
Nicole Flockton: Guarding Erin
Nicole Flockton: Guarding Suzie
Nicole Flockton: Guarding Brielle
Casey Hagen: Shielding Nebraska
Casey Hagen: Shielding Harlow
Casey Hagen: Shielding Josie
Casey Hagen: Shielding Blair
Desiree Holt: Protecting Maddie
Kathy Ivan: Saving Sarah
Kathy Ivan: Saving Savannah
Kathy Ivan: Saving Stephanie
Jesse Jacobson: Protecting Honor
Jesse Jacobson: Fighting for Honor
Jesse Jacobson: Defending Honor
Jesse Jacobson: Summer Breeze
Silver James: Rescue Moon
Silver James: SEAL Moon
Silver James: Assassin's Moon
Silver James: Under the Assassin's Moon
Becca Jameson: Saving Sofia
Kate Kinsley: Protecting Ava
Heather Long: Securing Arizona
Heather Long: Guarding Gertrude

Heather Long: Protecting Pilar
Heather Long: Covering Coco
Gennita Low: No Protection
Kirsten Lynn: Joining Forces for Jesse
Margaret Madigan: Bang for the Buck
Margaret Madigan: Buck the System
Margaret Madigan: Jungle Buck
Margaret Madigan: December Chill
Rachel McNeely: The SEAL's Surprise Baby
Rachel McNeely: The SEAL's Surprise Bride
Rachel McNeely: The SEAL's Surprise Twin
KD Michaels: Saving Laura
KD Michaels: Protecting Shane
KD Michaels: Avenging Angels
Wren Michaels: The Fox & The Hound
Wren Michaels: The Fox & The Hound 2
Wren Michaels: Shadow of Doubt
Wren Michaels: Shift of Fate
Wren Michaels: Steeling His Heart
Kat Mizera: Protecting Bobbi
Mary B Moore: Force Protection
LeTeisha Newton: Protecting Butterfly
LeTeisha Newton: Protecting Goddess
LeTeisha Newton: Protecting Vixen
LeTeisha Newton: Protecting Heartbeat
MJ Nightingale: Protecting Beauty
MJ Nightingale: Betting on Benny
MJ Nightingale: Protecting Secrets
Sarah O'Rourke: Saving Liberty
Debra Parmley: Protecting Pippa
Lainey Reese: Protecting New York

Jenika Snow: Protecting Lily
Jen Talty: Burning Desire
Jen Talty: Burning Kiss
Jen Talty: Burning Skies
Jen Talty: Burning Lies
Jen Talty: Burning Heart
Megan Vernon: Protecting Us
Megan Vernon: Protecting Earth

Fire and Police: Operation Alpha World

Freya Barker: Burning for Autumn
KaLyn Cooper: Justice for Gwen
Aspen Drake: Sheltering Emma
Barb Han: Kace
Reina Torres: Justice for Sloane
Stacey Wilk: Stage Fright

As you know, this book included at least one character from Susan Stoker's books. To check out more, see below.

SEAL of Protection: Legacy Series

Securing Caite

Securing Brenae (novella) (April 2019)

Securing Sidney (May 2019)

Securing Piper (Sept 2019)

Securing Zoey (TBA)

Securing Avery (TBA)

Securing Kalee (TBA)

Delta Force Heroes Series

Rescuing Rayne (FREE!)

Rescuing Aimee (novella)

Rescuing Emily

Rescuing Harley

Marrying Emily

Rescuing Kassie

Rescuing Bryn

Rescuing Casey

Rescuing Sadie

Rescuing Wendy

Rescuing Mary

Rescuing Macie (April 2019)

Badge of Honor: Texas Heroes Series

Justice for Mackenzie (FREE!)

Justice for Mickie

Justice for Corrie

Justice for Laine (novella)
Shelter for Elizabeth
Justice for Boone
Shelter for Adeline
Shelter for Sophie
Justice for Erin
Justice for Milena
Shelter for Blythe
Justice for Hope
Shelter for Quinn
Shelter for Koren (July 2019)
Shelter for Penelope (Oct 2019)

SEAL of Protection Series

Protecting Caroline (FREE!)
Protecting Alabama
Protecting Fiona
Marrying Caroline (novella)
Protecting Summer
Protecting Cheyenne
Protecting Jessyka
Protecting Julie (novella)
Protecting Melody
Protecting the Future
Protecting Kiera (novella)
Protecting Dakota

New York Times, *USA Today* and *Wall Street Journal* Bestselling Author Susan Stoker has a heart as big as the state of Tennessee where she lives, but this all American girl has also spent the last fourteen years living in

Missouri, California, Colorado, Indiana, and Texas. She's married to a retired Army man who now gets to follow *her* around the country.

She debuted her first series in 2014 and quickly followed that up with the SEAL of Protection Series, which solidified her love of writing and creating stories readers can get lost in.

If you enjoyed this book, or any book, please consider leaving a review. It's appreciated by authors more than you'll know.

www.stokeraces.com
www.AcesPress.com
susan@stokeraces.com

Printed in Great Britain
by Amazon

63348550R00171